THE GOOD DEITY

BOOK ONE
ALMOST COUNTABLE

OUTLANDERS OF THE MULTIVERSE
COLLECTION

BY D.N. LEO

Narrative Land Publishing
Narrativeland.com

**For a limited time, D.N. Leo gives away
4 books in the Multiverse Collection**

CLICK THE LINK AND CLAIM YOUR BOOKS
http://narrativeland.com

THANK YOU FOR READING!
D.N. LEO

THE GOOD DEITY

Almost Countable

Almost Sure

Almost Everywhere

The Good Deity - Almost Countable - Book 1
http://narrativeland.com/deity

Synopsis

Mya Portman is a young deity who believes she can tell the difference between good and evil. She is confident that she can save one thousand innocent souls from an unnatural death, and she has bet her freedom on it. A thousand years later, she is still working off the debts.

Now she is given an opportunity to pay off her debts. The only condition is that, for once, she has to turn a blind eye on some cases and allow people to die. Her record suggests that she will fail to look away again. But this time, it isn't just an opportunity to pay off her debt, it might be her Goddess's ultimatum.

This first installment in an urban fantasy, supernatural suspense series, filled with twists and turns, will make you question what you take for granted in this modern world.

PART ONE

CHAPTER 1

Once upon a time, there was a young deity who believed she could tell the difference between good and evil.

Her mother had told her never to put all of her eggs in one basket. Mya winced, looking at the scene in front of her. Maybe it wasn't her mother who said that, but that was beside the point. She was a young deity on her first mission to Earth, and she aimed to score big.

Now her basket of eggs was tumbling down the hill.

Literally.

From the top of the hill, Mya looked down the hillside and saw her way to hell.

The roar of the soldiers, thirsty for blood and hungry for victory, tore through the air of the dark rock valley. Swarms of black-clad riders and foot soldiers from the Wangi tribe raced forward to kill. The bright sunlight flashed onto their swords and scimitars, but it didn't infuse them with the guidance of humanity.

Mya watched the ruthless Wangi soldiers charge at a group of unprepared soldiers from the Glaixi tribe who were celebrating the peace treaty Mya had convinced the two tribes to sign.

"Nadinn! Cheater! Traitor! Coward!" Mya scolded and stormed down the hill, running toward the Glaixi's camp.

She didn't need to alert the soldiers as the roar of the opponents had sent all the Glaixi soldiers to their feet, grabbing their weapons wherever they could find them. She raced toward the tents of women and children, more than two thousand of them.

A few days ago, she thought she had scored a victory by helping the two tribes to sign the peace treaty. She thought she had saved the lives of those women and children that would otherwise be lost to war.

Spurred on by how the opposing army had turned into a chaotic mess, the Wangi soldiers rode on faster, yelling their battle cries as they galloped closer. They could smell blood as well as taste victory.

Mya ran faster. As a minor deity, people might have thought her Goddess would have given her the magnificent power to move mountains. But no—all she could do at the moment was run like the wind.

But at the moment, she didn't think she would be fast enough.

She ran faster and faster as the roar of the soldiers and the scream and clash of weapons erupted in the peaceful valley. By using her deity power to run this fast, she had violated the rule for the mission. But she no longer cared. She had to stop the soldiers.

Innocent women and children. More than two thousand of them waiting in tents for their Glaixi soldiers to return home from the battlefield after the celebration. Now that moment would never come.

"Stop!" she cried and darted in front of a group of Wangi soldiers who were about to rush into the camp to slaughter. "This tribe is under my protection. Turn back now or suffer my wrath!" Mya held her stance as the soldiers of the Wangi army looked at her with measured glances.

She was young. She had never been to battle. And she was dressed to attend the celebration in the valley. The golden leaves on her necklace were tangled in her hair, and eggshells and egg yolks were smeared on her hands from trying to catch them when the basket of food she'd brought for the party had tumbled down the hill.

But still, she would fight these soldiers to her death to save those innocent souls in the camp.

Nadinn, the leader, approached from a distance and dismounted his black warhorse.

"You've killed the soldiers. Please be merciful to the women and children." Mya tried to maintain a calm voice.

"These children will grow up to be the Glaixi tribe's soldiers, and they will then come after our tribe's children. I cannot put the future of my tribe at risk," Nadinn said, nodding at his soldiers as they stormed toward the camp to execute the ritualistic slaughter.

Mya drew out a small jar of potion and grabbed for Nadinn. "If I drop this jar, we will both die. I would rather die here than go back with a failed mission. Tell your soldiers to stop the killing."

Nadinn tried to shove Mya off of him, but he encountered one of her quirks—once she set her mind on something, she latched on like a leech. She wouldn't let go.

"Who do you serve? Who are you? Why are you doing this?" Nadinn snarled.

"I serve my Goddess, and she will not be pleased to see innocent people die. You don't want to suffer her wrath."

Nadinn laughed. "The Gods have abandoned us for many years. We have to take care of ourselves. This land can hold only one tribe. For many years, the Glaixi never let their guard down. We could never defeat them. We have to kill them now. This is our only chance."

"I convinced them to sign the treaty with you. I made them promises of God's favors. You're telling me I helped you to cheat and then slaughter these people?"

"Stay with us. You will have all you want."

"You've betrayed God. You've acted against God's will. You and your people will be punished."

"Maybe God has already been angry with my tribe, and that's why we suffered. That's why our children died of hunger. Or maybe God has simply been unfair to us."

"The Goddess is always fair and just."

Nadinn laughed—a crooked laugh. "The Glaixi had all the hunting grounds. They possessed all the water. We had nothing. We had to watch our women and children die. I've never spoken to your God in person. I only see you. The same with those who died today. They don't know why you do what you do, but for them, the blood is on your hands."

"I arranged the peace treaty so no one had to die!" she shouted.

"If they don't die, we will. Either way, the blood debt is on you. It will come back and haunt you one day," Nadinn said and hit Mya's hand away. The jar of potion dropped to the ground. White smoke streamed out from its broken lid.

In front of her was an explosion of whiteness. That was all she remembered.

CHAPTER 2

Mya pushed herself up on her elbows. The coldness of the marble floor seeped through her bare skin. The fabric that used to be her clothes was now tattered and soaked in blood—her blood.

Her long raven black hair was tangled like a poorly woven carpet and dangled down her shoulders, covering half of her face. She tucked the hair back behind her ear and looked at her reflection on the floor engraved with shiny gold floral etchings. She was lying in the middle of the Babylonian court—she was sure of it. She had spent endless days of her childhood polishing this floor.

Tap. Tap. Tap.

She looked up. Ishtar, the Goddess of love and war, was sitting on her throne, tapping her long nails on the arm of the chair and looking down at her with a smile that an ordinary person would consider gracious.

But Mya knew a storm was coming her way.

"Well, now I can finally get on with my court and take care of important matters. I thought you would lie there forever."

Mya scrambled up to her knees. "I beg your pardon, my Goddess."

Ishtar picked up a golden scroll from a tray and rolled out a thin silk report. "You saved one thousand and five innocent souls at the cost of two thousand one hundred and six innocent deaths. In addition, you cost me an extra dose of immortal potion because you let the human kill you. What do you have to say?"

"Please forgive me, my Goddess. I deserve to die. But I beg you not to send me to Hell Gate." Tears rolled down her face. There was no part of her body that was not aching at the moment. But the most painful part was the stench of blood that soaked the ground from those innocents she couldn't save.

"Give me a reason not to. You are afraid to see those sinful souls you killed? Then you should not have killed them!" Ishtar raised her voice—a rare occurrence.

Mya knew Ishtar adored her. She had disappointed her Goddess.

"You know I am fond of you. That was the only reason I gave you a chance to redeem your unforgivable mistake. To give you that chance, I had to defend you in front of other Gods and Goddesses. I assured them you wouldn't make a habit of this type of behavior. Maybe I was wrong. Your mistake can never be rectified."

"No, you weren't wrong. Please give me another chance. I'll redeem myself."

"You make one mistake after another. You give me no confidence in you at all. Give me a reason not to send you to Hell Gate."

Mya cried. "You're right. I deserve to go to Hell Gate, my Goddess."

Ishtar straightened her already-straight posture and appeared to calm down. Her eyes softened a bit. But a chill still ran up and down Mya's spine. She could never completely predict her Goddess's temperament.

"I wager it's natural that you chose to save one thousand innocent souls rather than kill one thousand sinful souls. Your choice reflects your good nature. But as you can see, the mission was not as easy as you thought. And I don't have the time and the people to rescue you whenever you fail."

"Give me another chance. Let me try. Please, my Goddess."

"I have to get you out of my sight. I will now send you back to Earth. You will not come back to court until you fulfill your mission. You will not receive any help from me or from my court. You will not have any power except for your natural talent. And if you let yourself kill again, there will not be another immortal potion for you. You will die like a mortal."

My natural talent? As far as she was concerned, she had only been good at two things in her life—she could run very fast, and she could scuffle. *Were they considered talents?* she wondered.

"Are you displeased?" Ishtar's voice rang like bell down the seemingly endless steps from her throne.

"No, my Goddess. I just don't know how to show my gratitude."

Ishtar nodded. "Good. I like you, so here is how I can help. I will give you a list of those to save. If you stick to the list and save those one thousand innocent souls, then you will be back to court in no time at all. Leon will go with you as a liaison from court. I hope to see you back in my chamber soon."

"Yes, of course, my Goddess. Thank you for your kindness."

CHAPTER 3

One thousand and fifteen years later.

Mya walked down the long hall of the Babylonian temple, heading toward the main court. She had lost count of how many times Ishtar had summoned her back to scold her for the negative balance between the people she should have but couldn't save and those she shouldn't have but did kill.

This time, it was different. The call had been urgent. She hadn't had any time to prepare and had no idea what was coming at her. One thing she knew for sure—her scorecard balance was way off. How much, she had no clue. She hadn't been keeping careful records.

There were only so many failures her Goddess would tolerate. Mya might lose her head this time. The scene of her head being chopped off and rolling across the shiny golden floor played over and over in her mind.

Mya looked down, counting her footsteps and listening to the sound of her heels clicking on the hard floor.

"Oh damn!" she almost shrieked out loud. Her soft voice echoed off of the golden flooring and walls, and she cringed as it bounced around and ended up back inside her own ears.

She'd forgotten to change before she left Earth.

In her human form, she was Professor Mya Portman, Professor of Mythology at a university. She had been on her way to a lecture when she'd been summoned. She had scrambled into a nearby closet and closed her eyes, and here she was at the ancient Babylonian Court of the Gods, dressed in her smart, corporate suit.

"Mylittle! Mylittle!" a voice called out.

Mya was startled and whirled around. She found Leon standing next to one of the golden pillars covered in golden leaves and vines. He grinned until he saw the expression on her face. He recoiled.

Leon was the head of the temple guard. He was a handsome man with light golden hair and eyes that sparkled. Mya had wondered about his position more than once as there didn't seem to be an ounce of toughness in him.

"How many times have I told you not to call me Mylittle?" she snarled.

Leon stared at her blankly. She stared back. Then she realized she had spoken to him in English. She had sunk so deeply into the vision of her head leaving her body that she'd forgotten that English wasn't the language spoken here. She repeated her statement in the Babylonian tongue of the Goddesses.

He didn't have a chance to answer her snide comment before she continued, "Take me to your chamber."

"What?" he blushed.

She gestured at her outfit. "I forgot to change."

He let out a sound of understanding, or maybe it was a sound of disappointment. She neither knew nor cared. Leon led the way to his chamber, which was nearby. As soon as he closed the door, she shrugged out of her clothes and put on the court outfit she always carried in her gigantic handbag—a golden bikini with dangling gold beads and golden leaves and other decorative items that only her Goddess Ishtar knew the significance of.

Her appearance changed a bit with the change of the outfit. Her hair grew longer and wavier and, like everything else in Babylon, it too held a touch of gold, and her skin bloomed with shimmering copper and gold.

Mya slipped on her golden sandals and shoved her suit into her gigantic handbag. While her hand was in the bag, she felt her cell phone buzz. The vibration startled her.

She was at the Babylonian temple, a place that didn't actually exist in current human civilization. She had no idea how her travel between the two worlds worked or where the two worlds were physically located. Every time she needed to travel, she simply closed her eyes, concentrated, and channeled the path to her court. She did the same on the return trip.

Well, they must be pretty close by! Mya rolled her eyes. This was the first time she had taken any belongings from the modern world to the court. Perhaps she should give her Goddess Ishtar a cell phone. It would certainly save a lot of back and forth travel.

She pulled out the phone and looked at the screen. There was a text message that said, *"Dan Chandler is in danger. Death by fire."*

"Oh hell!" Mya moaned. She cared for Dan. He was one of the very decent men she had come across on Earth. After the disastrous failure in the valley, she no longer took big cases. She stuck with Ishtar's list, handled each subject carefully, and hoped her scores trickled in enough to make her balance of a thousand souls. Because she handled subjects individually, she got to know them well.

She didn't like all of them, but Dan was one of those rare cases she genuinely cared about.

She had to save him. There was no time to see the Goddess. She closed her eyes, concentrated, and transported back to Earth.

CHAPTER 4

Lucas leaned back in his leather chair and put his feet on the desk. He closed his eyes and immersed his mind in his favorite Tchaikovsky concerto. The music washed over him, a storm of melody like the drama of his life.

He opened his eyes and looked at the check on the desk—a deposit for the job he had just taken. It was like God had finally heard his prayers.

He killed for a living, and he was good at his job. He was an excellent citizen as far as he was concerned. He had a legitimate business as a facade, and he paid taxes religiously on those business activities. He would be happy to pay tax on his assassin business as well, but he suspected the government wouldn't want blood money, so he kept the money for himself.

When he saved enough money, he'd retire and have a nice family. He would send his children to good schools, and they would, later on, contribute to society.

Lucas didn't know what had happened, but recently jobs had dried out. He didn't think the world had become more peaceful and people had suddenly decided to do the right thing and stop killing each other. On the contrary, the level of crimes and accidents reported on TV was higher than ever.

The only explanation he could think of was that ordinary people these days had become so skilled in killing that they could take on the task themselves, leaving professionals like him jobless.

He needed the money, and this contract had come at just the right time. Not only that, it was an easy and lucrative one.

***

Mya transported back to the closet at the university from which she had left Earth. She scrambled back to her office and darted to her desk phone.

"Sam, I have to leave. I have a family emergency. Can you take the class?"

"The introductory class?"

"Yes, there isn't much content at all. It's just an introduction."

"Sure, I know that, Mya... Are you okay?" Sam's voice sounded hesitant on the phone. He had been her assistant for three terms. He was competent. She never had to give him much instruction on her teaching tasks.

"Yes, I'm fine. Thanks for doing this. I owe you one." She hung up the phone then grabbed her bag and stormed out of the office, running right into Sam.

"Sam, I thought you were going to head over to my class," she said in a winded voice.

"You hung up the phone too quickly, Mya. You have to give me the teaching notes."

"Oh, yes. Of course." She pasted a quick smile on her face. "I'm sorry. Feeling scattered today. I have an emergency to attend to." She darted back into her office, grabbed the notes, and shoved them at Sam, "Here you are."

Sam was looking at her like she'd grown a second head.

"What's the problem?" She arched an eyebrow.

His wide eyes scanned her body, and when they made it back up to her face, he said, "Your outfit is...interesting."

Mya looked down. She was still in her golden bikini. She rolled her eyes and snorted.

She was tall, slim, and exotic. Exotic was the description she got all the time from male humans on Earth. Whenever they laid their eyes on her, not knowing she was a thousand-year-old deity and could read their thoughts when she was in her deity mode, the word exotic popped into their heads liked a neon billboard.

Her experience with humans had taught her that being exotic meant attractive, skewing slightly toward naughtiness, different from the common standards of beauty. Sam was one of the male humans who obsessed over her exotic beauty. Sometimes she wondered how he got any work done at all as much time as his mind spent concentrating on her.

She didn't have time to explain it to him right now, and she really didn't care if he thought she was coming from a sexy costume party in the middle of the day where they performed rituals and held orgies. She had a life and death situation to attend to.

She shoved him out the door and put on her running clothes. Before she left the office, she heard a 'gong.' That was the sound of someone trying to contact her from the court at the temple.

"Come on, not now!" she growled.

An image of Leon appeared, hovering in the air. "Mya! You left the court before seeing the Goddess. She's very angry."

"She sent you here to get me?"

"No. I sneaked out. Come on. Come back to court. There's something going on there. That's why she summoned you."

"Not now. I have to save a subject. I'll come back when I'm finished."

"It's only a subject, Mya. Your life is on the line—"

"Stuff that, Leon. A subject is a life I care about. If I don't care, what the hell have I been doing for the last thousand years?"

"Mya!"

"Tell Ishtar I will see her as soon as my subject is safe and sound."

"Don't do this..."

Mya arched an eyebrow.

Leon nodded. "I'll do my best to calm Ishtar."

"You don't have to do anything for me. Playing with Ishtar's temper is dangerous. Just tell her I put the life of my subject first, as always. I understand she has important matters to see to. But the safety of my subjects is important, not only to me but for her reputation as well."

"I can't let anything happen to you, Mya."

"Nothing will. She needs me here, Leon."

Leon shook his head. "I won't let her harm you..." His image faded away.

"Don't— Damn it!" Mya cursed but was sure Leon didn't hear, nor would he have understood because she cursed in English.

Save Dan first. Mya concentrated. She turned on her deity mode, and then she could run like the wind. She stormed out the door.

CHAPTER 5

She could smell the smoke flooding her nostrils as she came close to the building where Dan worked. She looked up to see it rolling in the sky like black clouds on their way in for a big storm. When she moved even closer, she could see that chaos had ensued around the building. Fire trucks and police cars were all over, and emergency personnel had the area roped off as they went about trying to rescue those inside. There were people gathered around outside, some of them praying that their loved ones would be the next brought out and some practically incapacitated by the torrents of tears that racked their bodies.

Mya used her supernatural abilities to block out all of the sounds so that she could scan the scene without interruption. Everything slowed down as she ran her eyes across the building, searching inside for her subject. She could see through the people and the trucks and the building. She could connect in a psychic way with her subject once she found him.

Dan was at the far end of the building. When she found him, she closed her eyes and concentrated, waiting for the signals. She could hear his heartbeat, slow, steady, and most importantly, alive. She could see him now in a room at the far end of the building. He was lying on the floor, not moving. He was obviously unconscious. She took in all the sights and sounds and smells in the room. A heavy odor floated about. Mya sniffed, and panic seized her—the smell was gas. Her eyes moved back to the front of the building where the fire raged. That was where the rescues were taking place. There was no fire yet at Dan's end of the building, so there were no uniforms there.

Mya was going to have to get him out of there herself. That would mean switching off her powers and going in to save him like a human. Otherwise, the rescue wouldn't even count. She took a deep breath, concentrating on all of the visual and sensory information one last time. Then she closed her eyes and switched off her supernatural abilities.

Even as an ordinary human, Mya was quick on her feet. She darted toward the far end of the building and entered from the parking lot. Everyone's attention was currently concentrated on the commotion at the other end of the building, leaving this part unattended.

She heard the faint sound of singing as she sprinted through the empty lot and into the building. She looked around to get her bearings. The smell of gas filled her nose and her human lungs. She could still hear the singing. It was a soft voice, and it echoed down the corridor. It was something soothing and pretty like a lullaby, not in English but in a language Mya didn't instantly recognize.

"Hello?" she called out. The only answer was the sound of her own voice bouncing along the walls. She located the room where she had seen Dan and tried the door. It was locked. She looked around the hall, and her eyes fell on the glass cabinet of a fire emergency compartment. She shouldered the glass, and as it shattered and cascaded to the floor, she grabbed the hammer inside. She took it and hit the door handle as hard as she could. The hammer only bounced, sending numbing vibrations all the way to her shoulder.

"Damn it!" she muttered, suddenly remembering that she was an ordinary human now. Summoning all of her strength, she raised the hammer and brought it back down on the handle.

This time, it gave way. She kicked the door in and stormed into the room. It was a storage room, small and filled with gas fumes. The open door provided an inlet for the fresh air and an outlet for the gas. The rush of clean air caused Dan to stir. Mya covered her mouth and nose with one of her sleeves as she darted toward him.

"Dan! Can you hear me?" She tapped lightly on his face.

He'd gone still and silent again. She tapped his shoulder then and asked once more, "Dan, it's Mya. Can you hear me?"

He didn't respond. They needed to get out of there. Holding her breath, she tucked her arms underneath Dan's from the behind and dragged him outside the room into the hall.

There was still no one around. This part of the building was completely isolated. She had no help now. Dan was breathing, but he was dead weight. She couldn't carry him outside the building.

She heard the singing again and looked up to see a young Asian girl sitting on the ledge outside the balcony of the parking garage. Her legs dangled, and her long hair flowed out into the wind. Suddenly her big eyes darkened, and she stared straight at Mya with an absent expression. Her lips continued to move, and the sound that flowed out hung on the wind. It was a lullaby.

The hair on the back of Mya's neck stood up, and she shouted at the girl, "Get down from there!"

The girl kept singing.

At first, Mya worried that when the fire reached her, the girl would panic and jump from the building. But the more she looked at her, the more she realized that the girl didn't look human. She looked more like a spirit...a ghost.

"Get down! Can you hear me?" Mya tried again. There was still no reaction from the girl. Mya turned her attention back to her charge on the floor.

"Dan, please answer me," she said with desperation in her voice.

He stirred again.

"Oh my God, come on, wake up!" She shook his shoulders. There was still no response, so she shook him a little more violently.

Dan grumbled and opened his eyes.

"Dan, Dan, can you hear me? Can you see me?" He nodded. "Thank God!" Mya said, helping him up to a sitting position.

They heard the singing again, and Dan looked up. Still disoriented, he jumped to his feet then staggered and slumped down again.

"Riko! What are you doing? Come down here!" he yelled.

The girl he called Riko kept whispering that strange lilting song. Mya helped Dan stand. He swayed and leaned against the wall for balance.

"Riko!" Dan called out again.

"We need to get out of here, Dan. You smell the gas?" Mya asked.

Dan snapped back to reality but still looked at Riko.

"She came to my office and stood there with a strange look on her face. Then she started walking down the hall like she was in a trance...like a zombie. I called out and followed her. The next thing I know, I woke up with you slapping at my face."

They heard a squeaking sound from the door at the end of the corridor. Mya raced to the doorway and watched as their only way of escape slammed shut.

"Damn! She lured you here. We have to get out of here. How many other exits are there?"

"That was the only one." Dan gestured toward the closed door, panic beginning to color his face.

"What the hell is going on? Who wants you dead, Dan?"

He shook his head and winced. In the dim light of the corridor, blood streamed from his right leg and pooled on the floor.

"I don't know..."

"You're injured," Mya said, crouching to take a look.

"We have to get out of here. Gas is everywhere. It'll only take one spark to send us into oblivion," Dan said.

"The other end of the building is on fire," she told him.

"What? Okay," Dan puffed, trying to keep his composure, "this is definitely a setup, although I'm not sure killing me will benefit anyone. I'm just an accountant. I balance other people's money, but I don't have any more than my salary. Why would anyone want to kill me?" He turned around, back toward Riko, and said to her, "If you don't get down, we'll leave you here, Riko. Zach won't come for you this time."

"What?" Mya asked.

Dan shook his head. The girl kept singing.

"Dan!" They heard Zach's voice echoing from outside.

"Oh, crap!" Dan said as he realized what was happening. "Holy crap. This wasn't for me. The setup was for Zach."

CHAPTER 6

Smoke had fumed out from the other corridor. The heat and the smell of gas had intensified. Mya cursed. Both Dan and Zach were on her list to protect. But Zach's profile had never been flagged. If she had known she would have to rescue them both, she would have been better prepared. Mya grabbed at Dan's arm.

"Do you mean someone wants to kill Zach?"

"They've tried before. We got out of it. It's a long story."

"Dan!" Zach called again.

Dan limped toward the door. "In here. But don't come in! We'll come out."

"Let me," Mya slid her arm around's Dan's waist to help him walk. The smell of gas was growing stronger by the second. Dan looked back at Riko and tried once more, "Riko, come on."

They heard the door swing open as Zach broke the handle. Zach stormed in and bolted toward them.

"Professor Portman," he said, obviously surprised to see her.

"Which part of don't come in here did you not understand?" Dan exclaimed.

"All of it, but there was no way you were coming out otherwise. What's wrong with your leg?" Zach asked.

"Zach, there's a girl sitting outside." Mya pointed to the ledge above.

Zach looked up and saw Riko. He stared at her. Mya expected him to call out to her, but he merely grimaced. He took a stance as if bracing himself against an invisible attacker and then narrowed his eyes at Riko. Mya wished she could slide into her deity skin to read Zach's thoughts. But she had to stay human until Dan was safe.

As Zach stared, the girl stopped singing. Her image flickered, and then she disappeared.

Mya wished again she could switch back to deity mode to find out what was going on, but there was no time, and it wasn't an important matter at the moment.

"Professor Portman," Zach said again.

"Huh?"

"That wasn't Riko. It was a hologram. It's a long story, and I'll explain later. Can we get out of here now? The place reeks of gas." Zach grabbed Dan's arm to help him walk.

As soon as they started moving, Mya saw a movement from the corner of her eye. She looked in that direction and saw a girl of about five years of age. She had wandered in from another wing of the building. Her little face was as pale as a ghost, and she looked like she was too shocked to even be frightened.

"You take Dan out of the building," Zach said. "I'll go back for the girl."

"No, Zach, Dan's heavier than the kid. I can handle this. You keep going," Mya told him.

She dashed back toward the girl as hundreds of scenarios flashed through her mind. It was like watching a reel of a bad movie. She had done this so many times—saving the wrong people. She knew Dan's files. He would live until the end of his natural life and die from natural causes. Anything that ended his life now would be unnatural, and it was her duty to save him from an unnatural death. But she didn't have the girl's file. She didn't have time to check the girl's natural life span. She had to be in her deity form to pull that information. If the girl was meant to finish this life and move on to the next, Mya's interference would be a negative mark against her record.

Zach turned back and saw that Mya had stopped running,

"Professor Portman, please take Dan. I'll go back for the girl."

She couldn't let Zach go back. It was too dangerous. His safety was her top priority. He saw her hesitance over saving the girl, but she knew he didn't understand her situation. He might think she was scared—which would be natural for a human given the occasion but was an insult to Mya. He would judge her, and for some reason unknown even to her, his opinion of her was important. She would have to save the girl, whether dying today was her fate or not. She would have to deal with the consequences of it later.

"Damn it!" she muttered as she made her way down the corridor. She approached the girl quickly, scooped her up, and ran back the other way.

Zach and Dan were outside the building, and Mya was nearly at the door when she heard a *swoofff*. The pressure from the gas explosion pumped through the corridor and shot Mya and the girl outside like a missile.

They rolled on gravel and cement, Mya trying to cover the girl as much as possible, tasting the saltiness of the blood in her mouth. She knew now what the expression "seeing stars" meant. She felt the cold air biting at her skin through the tears in her clothing, poking heavily at the injuries she hadn't yet had time to assess. A terrible pain sliced through her mind, and she decided that being human sucked. Then her world went black.

***

Lucas threw the bottle of beer at the computer screen and roared in frustration. "Who the fuck is Zach Flynn?"

Alice hugged him from behind. They had been together for a long time, and she was always there for him when he needed her. Lucas was aware of that. He hadn't promised her anything, but when it was time to build a family, she was the one he planned to spend the rest of his life with.

"Shhh, calm down, Lucas. We'll sort this out." Her smooth voice always comforted him.

"How?" He turned and looked at her. "I can't see a way out. I've taken the deposit. We promised to kill Dan. I should never have taken this stupid job. Why can't I just put a bullet in the guy's head? Why does it have to be under the girl's watch? Who is she? I can kill her, too, as a bonus!"

She pressed a finger to his lips to silence him. "No, you'll violate your own rules. That's no good for business, and it's unprofessional. Never question a client. Remember? Whatever they want, we'll do it for money. I do have good news, and I hope it lightens your mood."

Lucas turned and looked into Alice's deep brown eyes. "I'd love to hear it."

"The dealer said the contractor understands the situation and didn't ask for his money back. On the contrary, he'll double the payment if we can take Zach out as well."

Lucas grinned. "Why didn't you say so earlier?"

Alice smiled. "Gotta let you sweat a bit. Zach Flynn's interference isn't our fault. We didn't have the information."

Lucas frowned. "I hate working on cases when we don't have the full picture."

Alice laughed. "I disagree. Unless we're paid more, I don't want to know more than we need to know to do the job."

"That's my girl." Lucas pinched Alice's cheek lightly, then he kissed her. But the passionate kiss didn't clear the knot that tangled in his mind about this deal. This wasn't his first job, but it was the first untidy one. He disliked loose ends because experience had told him they'd come back and bite him in the backside.

CHAPTER 7

Mya woke in a hospital bed, confused and disoriented at first. She looked around, her eyes finally landing on Zach sleeping in a chair in a corner. He had sunk down in the chair with his head tilted in an uncomfortable position. He was going to have a sore neck later. His long legs stretched out on the floor, and Mya could see he was exhausted. His brilliant and witty green eyes were closed now, but she would love to see them smile at her later. His slightly long brown hair was disheveled and had fallen across the front of his forehead.

She looked at his strong jaw and his unshaven face then moved her eyes to his lips. Something about them made her want to taste them and savor their fullness.

She shook her head. *Stop it, Mya! What if he wakes up to find a deity drooling sinfully over him? You'll have no dignity left at all.*

It was time for her to take inventory. She shifted and slid down under the blanket so that if Zach woke, he would not see what she was doing. In her deity form, she knew her eyes looked a bit glassy. It might be considered spooky from a human perspective.

In her deity form, she searched for the little girl's files.

"Oh, damn it. I knew this would happen!" she exclaimed. The girl was destined to finish this life. She had been a criminal in her previous life. She'd served a short life this time and was supposed to move on to be born a brilliant scientist in her next life. Because Mya had saved the girl, she'd interfered with God's plan. This one was going to cause a big ding on Mya's score card. It had been more than a thousand years, and she still hadn't learned to look away from people in need.

"Oh, crap. Shit. Shit. And triple shit," she cursed boldly underneath her blanket.

"Professor Portman?"

Mya heard Zach call out. She flipped the blanket down to reveal her face. "Don't call me Professor!"

Zach recoiled at her tone. "I'm sorry, Pro ... Mya. How are you feeling? Who would you like me to call?"

Why did he assume she had someone to call? Why didn't he just ask *if* there was someone to call? Not everyone had loving parents, understanding brothers, sisters, in-laws, nieces, nephews, and friends to die for or call for help from at any moment.

Yes, she had followed him to get the information. In her *profession*, following him was not considered stalking. Her Goddess had given her a long list this year to protect, and Zach's name was on it. So effectively, she was his guardian angel. She preferred that job title to deity, but beggars couldn't be choosers. She had been lucky to hang on to her job after so many centuries where she hadn't been able to fulfill the tasks Ishtar had given her.

She never had personal relationships with her subjects. It was a formula for disaster. A few months ago when she was bored out of her skull, she had gone to the club where Zach and his band played every weekend. A fan of his who had been sitting next to Mya threw her bra at him on the stage. There was nothing Mya could do when Zach thought she was the one who had thrown it.

Later, he had approached her table to thank her for her support. She had no choice but to explain that she wasn't the one who had tossed him the bra. Of course she followed up with, "Don't get me wrong, I do love your music. It was just that I wouldn't express my support the way your other fans do." She had given him her business card, and the next thing she knew, he turned up at the university asking for her help.

When he wasn't playing in the band, Zach gave guitar lessons at a small music school he founded. He wanted to know how he could bring some of his material to courses at the university. She couldn't help him much in that regard because (a) she was tone deaf and (b) she didn't have any real friends in the faculty due to her situation. But the interactions between Zach and her had started from there. They weren't exactly friends—that was obvious from the fact that Zach still called her Professor Portman.

"No, I don't know anyone here. If you could check me out of the hospital, though, that would be great," Mya said and sat up in her bed.

Zach nodded. "You were really brave, Pro ... Mya." *And attractive, and smart, and...*

"Oh no!" Mya shrieked out loud. She had left her deity vision on, thus she could hear Zach's thoughts. As much as she enjoyed it, it was totally unethical by her heavenly standards. Mya grabbed at her head and closed her eyes. Switched off.

She opened her eyes and saw Zach sitting on the end of her bed.

"Are you okay? I don't think you should check out of the hospital so soon. You were hit really hard. The doctor said you have a mild concussion. Look, if you don't want to call anyone, I'll stay until you're steady. But leaving you alone is not an option." He bit his lower lip, having more to say but trying not to say it.

"I'm fine."

"No, you're not."

"How are Dan and the kid?"

"They're both fine."

"I'm hungry."

"Huh?"

She arched an eyebrow. "A girl's gotta eat."

"Oh, right. I'm sorry. What would you like?"

"Wonton noodle soup with extra wontons and fewer noodles, a wedge of lemon, and some fresh chili with no fried onion."

"Ah...noted." Zach smiled and turned on his heel. As soon as he closed the door, Mya slid down in the bed, dropped her head back against the pillow, and started tallying her balance. She suddenly realized she had lost count of how many cases she was supposed to save to fulfill her original contract with her Goddess.

Not reading the fine print in the agreement had hurt her for more than a thousand years. She knew now that she wasn't allowed to kill anyone, including bad guys—a rule that she continually violated. She wasn't allowed to save those who were supposed to die. And there were a dozen more forbidden actions in the fine print. She wondered if there was an ultimatum clause—she had an odd feeling that there was.

She concentrated and tried to retrieve her original agreement. But all she had now was a blank document.

CHAPTER 8

The doctor insisted Mya stay in the hospital overnight for further observation. Against her own wishes, she agreed. Dan had been released the previous night, and he was an ordinary human being. She was a deity. How could he recover faster than her? As much as Mya thought it was unfair, she said nothing. Doctors and Gods were those she didn't argue with.

Zach was on his way to pick her up from the hospital and take her back to her apartment. He acted as if she couldn't hail a cab herself. But she couldn't prevent him from acting on his own will. Not to mention that the idea of being taken care of by Zach pleased her. She had never felt that kind of pleasure before. Her as-long-as-the-eternity life was all about taking care of others. It was nice to be tucked into bed and have someone bring her food and worry about her. And the fact that it was Zach taking care of her made it that much nicer.

In his music business, Zach was like a God to his fans. He looked like a God, and he performed like one. He could have any girl he wanted, but like her, Zach lived a double life. Despite his rock-star status, he was a well-loved man to his friends and family. During her *professional* observation, Mya had seen Zach taking care of the people he loved. He never brought his wild music business home. She had seen him visiting his parents often, bringing presents to his nieces and nephews, and being generous and kind to his friends and his students. It was a fair guess that he would be a wonderful father one day. Mya saw that he was a gentleman to his girlfriend, Chloe.

There was *that*, Mya thought with a sigh. His stunning childhood sweetheart. Just thinking about it made her heart ache.

"Stop it!" She smacked herself in the head. "You're two years his senior. Actually, a thousand years his senior. You're worse than a cougar. And a good deity does not have hormonal issues."

She heard the faint tinkle of a bell, and a hovering image of Leon appeared in the air above her.

"Wow." Mya stepped back and stared at him. She bit her tongue discreetly to ensure she said nothing. Something strange was happening. It felt as if a storm was coming her way.

"Mya, Ishtar has a message for you." Leon nodded slightly in greeting and spoke in English, a language he'd had no knowledge of as of yesterday.

"Double wow. Hi there. Since when has your job description changed? Don't tell me you broke a crystal and are about to be exiled like me?" Mya gasped.

Leon smiled and said, "I'm now in charge of Ishtar's communication to deities who work...remotely."

Mya rolled her eyes. "Yeah, I can see the position came with language capabilities. If she could give abilities to you so easily, why didn't she give me a superpower, too, so I could do my job faster?"

"I've been promoted. As you said, you were exiled. There's a difference in the amount of privileges one can get under those circumstances."

Mya's blood ran cold. This was a different Leon than the one who had blushed when she asked him to take her to his chamber. She shifted her stance, bracing herself for the coming news.

"What's the message?"

"Yesterday, you didn't make the meeting. Ishtar took a hundred points off your scorecard."

"That's a bit harsh. No, that's unreasonably harsh."

"Well, Ishtar thinks you didn't respect her time."

"I... All right, I'll make up the points. I don't even know how many points I have to make up!"

"Umm..."

"What?"

"You have seven days to bring your balance up to zero."

"I'm in the negative? How the hell will I ever make it to a thousand? And what the heck with the deadline? I've never had a deadline before. Don't I have to wait for people to be in danger to save them? I can't control that. And I don't know how many points I need to get to zero."

"Two."

Mya stared. "You checked my records? Hell, I don't even know my balance. What if I can't save two lives in seven days, Leon? What will happen? How will Ishtar punish me?"

"I'm not in a position to answer that question."

"What's going on at court, Leon?"

Leon shook his head, "I can't tell you, but...Ishtar is...restructuring her council and changing policies. That much I know. You have to be careful."

Mya nodded. She mumbled to herself, "Wartime." They had gone past the period of peace and prosperity, and Ishtar was the Goddess of love and war. Mya looked up and saw that Leon's image had disappeared.

CHAPTER 9

Lucas's blood boiled with anger. He had a feeling this luxurious office in the most exclusive high-rise building in the center of the Central Business District wouldn't have enough space to contain his ego. Especially when said ego was being damaged.

He slammed the phone down as his girlfriend, Alice, walked into his office.

"What's wrong?" she asked.

He frowned, looking her in the eye. "Have you ever talked to the client directly?"

"Which one?" Alice dropped down onto a comfortable reading chair.

"You know which one I'm talking about."

The smile faded from her face. "You're talking about the one who paid us an obscene amount of money to kill two guys? The accountant and the musician?" She arched an eyebrow.

"Don't be snide. You know it's not as easy as it sounds, Alice."

"I'm not stupid."

"Then answer me. I asked if you had ever talked to the client yourself. How did you find this client?"

"I went through a broker. Tell me what's going on, Lucas." She stood up.

Lucas looked pensively at the computer. "The client is sending help our way."

"Isn't that good? As long as he doesn't cut back on the payment."

Lucas shook his head. "Money isn't the issue. The people he's sending are the issue. We kill for a living. But we have our standards, Alice. The new people—they're not from here."

Alice scowled. "So what country are they coming from? As long as they speak English, it shouldn't be a problem."

Lucas shook his head. "I don't think they speak at all."

***

Mya's phone vibrated, and a text message appeared as she checked it. *"Dan Chandler is in danger. Death by fire."*

She furrowed her eyebrows. Didn't she rescue him just yesterday from a death by fire? It hadn't counted toward her balance because she had saved a girl she shouldn't have saved, but this had to be a mistake. She checked the time and date and was sure that this was a new message from her deity network.

Mya concentrated and switched to her deity vision. She saw Dan walking into a place that looked like an art exhibit of some kind. Around Dan were several paintings and sculptures. Where was he? Mya heard familiar footsteps and shook her head. She could hear and feel Zach now. He was very close by. Mya snapped back to reality and switched off her vision.

She opened the door of the room as soon as Zach arrived. Zach had his hand in the air as if he was about to knock. He smiled. "Are you a psychic?"

"What are you thinking about?" she responded.

Zach grinned. "I'm glad you're not one of those mind rapists."

"Psychic ability is a talent, Zach. I'm sure those with the talent wouldn't appreciate how you label them."

He shook his head and gestured her to follow him. "It's not a talent. It's a curse."

"Like you'd know." She snorted and followed him. She saw Zach's lips form a thin line, and it looked like a thought crossed his mind. But she needed her deity vision on to read his thoughts. Unable to do it now, she sighed and let her curious urges go.

Zach approached his motorbike parked around the corner, pulled out a spare helmet, and gave it to Mya. She stared at it.

"I hope you don't mind. The band is using my car to load new gear for the show tomorrow. I can get a cab if you prefer something that moves on four wheels."

Mya shook her head and grabbed the helmet. "No, this is fine."

***

Sitting behind Zach with her body pressed against his would normally be a thrill for Mya, but her mind was too busy now with the possibility that Dan might be burned to death somewhere.

"How's Dan this morning?"

"I just called him. He's fine. Back to work already."

"Where is he?"

"His company sponsors an art exhibition of some sort. He organizes the event. So he's at the Melbourne Art Center, doing his business nonsense."

"Can you take me there?"

"I'm going to meet up with him tonight. We have some important business to see to. You're welcome to join us for dinner—"

"Take me to Dan."

"I haven't asked you how you found out where Dan was yesterday and how you knew he was in trouble."

"Take me to the art center," Mya told him again, firmly. Her stomach fluttered. She knew Dan's danger was hovering nearby, but she didn't know exactly what it was. Zach asked nothing further. He made a U-turn and headed toward the highway.

CHAPTER 10

The exhibition was enormous. Artwork was displayed both inside and outside of a large, impressive building. People were everywhere. They poured in from a nearby tram stop and from around the botanical garden across the street. Both tourists and locals seemed to be enjoying a day out at the exhibition. The air was filled with the sound of chattering and laughing.

Mya scanned the crowd with her human eyes, but it didn't help much.

"Can you get any closer? I can't see Dan from here," she asked Zach. Then she saw the barricades and stop signs for general traffic. "Damn it. Forget about it, Zach. They don't allow traffic in."

"If you're sensing that Dan is in some kind of trouble, by the time we finish scanning this ground on foot, he'll probably be dead."

"Yes, but you're not allowed to drive in."

"Then we'll ride in," Zach said as he dodged his motorbike through a gap between the fences.

They circled the exhibition grounds a few times but couldn't find Dan. Security spotted them snaking around on the motorbike among the crowd.

"We might have to go into the exhibition hall," Mya said.

Zach glanced at the security guards who were speaking into their radios. "I agree," he said and turned the motorbike around to find a parking lot.

When they got to the exhibition hall, Mya couldn't control her agitation. She looked everywhere, scanning everyone's faces.

Zach pulled out his phone to call Dan. "He's on his damn phone." Then he looked at her. "Okay, I think it would be best if you tell me what's going on, Mya."

"Turn around. Don't look at me."

"No, I—"

"Turn around if you don't want Dan dead."

Zach stared at her then nodded and turned away. Mya switched to her deity vision. Zach turned back toward her and stared at her. She was aware of what she looked like when she was in deity mode, but she no longer cared. She needed to find Dan.

She blocked all the noise of the thousands of people out of her head and channeled Dan. She could hear him now, talking on his cell phone. She could hear his heartbeat, strong and healthy. She started walking toward it. She sensed Zach following her and felt him put his hand on the small of her back.

They weaved their way through the crowd, and after a few minutes, Mya said, "He's there," and pointed. Then she switched back to her human vision.

From a distance, Zach and Mya could see Dan still talking to someone on his cell phone.

"Oh no, look at that painting." A chill ran down Mya's spine.

Dan was approaching a large painting standing on an easel. It was a painting of a castle on fire. She charged toward Dan, calling out to him.

Dan didn't hear her, and he sauntered right in front of the painting. He turned around and saw them running toward him and heard them calling. The smile on his face faded suddenly, and then so did his image.

Dan dissolved into the air in front of the painting as if he had been sucked right into it.

Mya and Zach both watched it happen, but no one else saw it. Thousands of visitors, including those standing next to Dan, saw nothing.

Zach and Mya ran toward the painting.

"What the fuck? What's going on?" Zach looked at the painting and scanned the crowd frantically. "Did you see that, too, Mya, or was it just me?"

She nodded. "I saw it."

"So you... You're a psychic? You told me to come here. Can you tell me what else you saw? Where's Dan? Is he okay? I mean, is he alive?"

"Yes, he's alive."

Zach huffed. "He's obviously been swallowed up by this painting. But as long as he's alive, maybe I can yank him out. Are you sure he's alive?"

"What do you want to hear, Zach?"

Zach calmed down. "I'm sorry." He sat down on a nearby bench and grabbed his head. "If anything happens to him, it's my fault."

Mya sat down next to him and rested a hand on his back. "Why?"

Zach shook his head. "It's a long story. I have to get him out of there. I need to get him to a place where he's needed. It's very far away from here..."

Mya raised an eyebrow. From her perspective, there was no place as far away as the Babylonian court where she still served. But Zach wouldn't understand. So she said nothing.

Mya had her deity vision on, and she tried to reach Zach's thoughts. But for some reason, his thought process was patchy. She couldn't get a grip on it like she'd been able to before. Something in him had changed profoundly since the last time she had spoken to him, but she didn't know what. She switched her deity vision off.

Mya and Zach looked back at the painting. It had been replaced by a painting of a mountain landscape.

"What the heck?" Zach gasped. They rushed toward it.

"We've lost the painting. We've lost him!" Mya said.

"Thank you for visiting. You look like you enjoy my work." A man in his forties stood next to the painting and grinned at them.

Mya and Zach turned toward the voice.

"Where's the painting of the castle on fire?" Mya asked.

The artist frowned. "I'm afraid I don't have that one in my portfolio."

"Did you just sell it?" Zach asked.

"Oh no. I'm not that lucky. This blissful mountain has been here for a few days. I don't see that it's going anywhere now that the exhibition is coming to an end tomorrow. I don't have a castle painting. You must have seen it elsewhere." The artist sighed.

Zach looked around. It had been here, on this very easel. "Didn't we see it here, Mya?"

Mya nodded and walked toward a quiet corner. She turned, looked at a wall, and switched her deity vision on. Zach knew what she was doing, but he kept quiet and waited.

Mya scanned as she walked, and Zach followed. She heard Dan's heartbeats, still strong and steady. But she couldn't locate him now. There was no vision. The signals were distorted. She turned around and around until she became so disoriented she lost her balance. She almost fell into another painting when she felt Zach's arms around her.

"That's enough, Mya. Come back to me, please."

She wanted to, but she had to find Dan. She turned around and around. She saw nothing. She was dizzy, but she continued to whirl around, scanning, scanning, and scanning. She felt as if she had gone blind. She felt a tear roll down her face. Then she felt Zach's arms around her shoulders, his grip so strong she could no longer move.

"Stop turning around. Stay still."

Her body was pressed against Zach's, so closely she could hear his heartbeat and feel the warmth of his body. She smelled his aftershave, masculine and spicy. She stayed still until he sat her down on a bench and wiped a tear from her face.

"I'm sorry. I can't see him."

"As long as he's alive—"

"He is. I'm sure of it."

Zach lifted her chin up and looked into her eyes. "Can you turn off those glassy eyes? I want to see you again."

She switched off her deity vision.

"Why are you so concerned about Dan? You've barely known us for a few months."

"Are you suggesting I shouldn't be concerned about people dying even though I can see it in my vision?"

Zach nodded. "Fair enough. I'm sorry..." He trailed off and narrowed his eyes at a far corner of the exhibition ground. "The gateway," he said. He stood up and ran to the corner. Mya could see a strange layer of mist that made the air in the corner look like a smoking mirror.

She followed Zach, but he told her, "No, you stay here."

"The hell I will."

Zach kept moving toward the misty pool of air. "It's dangerous, Mya. You can get hurt."

"Then I won't let you go there alone. I have to protect you."

"What?"

Mya shrugged and didn't answer.

"Stay here. You don't know what's going on." Zach tried to rush away from her.

"You're the one who doesn't know what's going on," Mya protested.

Zach shook his head and charged straight into the middle of the mist. Mya followed.

They found themselves in a dungeon. Zach grabbed Mya and pushed her behind him.

"Dan!" Zach called out.

Mya switched her deity vision on to figure things out, but it didn't work. It was dark except for a dim, flickering light that came from nowhere. A cold breeze crept in, but there was no door or window in sight...which also meant no way out.

CHAPTER 11

On the left, there seemed to be a tunnel. Zach held Mya's hand, and they followed the smooth wall of the tunnel.

The faint sound of someone singing began to echo in the cold air and bounce off of the tunnel walls. The voice was soft and misty as if it rose from the floor. Mya recognized the song. It was the one the girl Riko had been singing from the ledge. Zach had referred to her as a hologram yesterday. But wouldn't light be needed to project a hologram? Mya wondered. It was dark here—no light and no hologram. Just the voice.

A wedge of deep blue light appeared in front of them, and within it stood Riko. The image wavered a bit, the blue light beams bent by the mist seeping out from the wall. The voice came out from the girl, but unlike yesterday, her mouth was not moving.

Zach did what he had done the day before. He concentrated and stared hard at Riko. Her image flickered, but it didn't go away this time. Zach grunted and staggered back, falling into Mya. It seemed like the girl had pushed Zach backward without even moving. Mya grabbed him and felt his body vibrate as if an electric current had passed through him. He was as cold as ice, and a drop of blood trickled from his nose. He kept staring at the girl's image as if firing a missile at her with his eyes.

Zach suddenly clenched his jaw, stood back up, and charged at the girl. The singing stopped, and a blanket of blue current wrapped around him, throwing him backward and smashing him against the wall close to the ceiling of the tunnel. His body slid down to the floor. He wiped away the blood coming from his nose and the corner of his mouth and pulled himself back up.

Mya charged at the girl. When he realized what she was going to do, Zach tried to grab her, but she slipped out of his grip. She picked up a loose brick from the ground and threw it at the girl's head. Blankets of blue current flew at Mya, wrapping her up, but they had no effect on her. Mya smiled. She picked up more bricks—and anything else she could get her hands on—and threw them at the image. Riko flickered a few times and then disappeared.

Mya returned to Zach. He was standing up, leaning against the wall. He grabbed her arms and checked her body. Mya didn't know what kind of damage the current had done to him because it had had no effect on her, but she could tell that Zach was in too much pain to talk.

"Can you walk, Zach?"

He nodded. She slid her arm around his waist for support. They took a couple of steps before a red wedge of light appeared in front of them. In the middle of the light stood an ugly half-zombie, half-ape creature.

"If you want to take an Earth form, try picking a better looking one," Zach muttered.

The creature sent a red blanket of light at them. Zach spun Mya around, not knowing that the current had no effect on her. The current hit him full force from behind. He slumped to the floor. Mya searched around on the dark ground for something she could use as a weapon and found what felt like a metal bar. She grabbed it, charged at the creature, and swung the bar.

The creature sent blankets of light at her but was stunned to see they had no effect on her. She didn't even suffer a scratch. Unlike the computer-generated image of Riko, this one seemed more real. It seemed to have substance and a thought process. With her deity vision, she could see images and text flowing out from the creature in the form of an electrical wave. It seemed like data was being processed.

A hollow voice croaked out from the creature. "Who are you?"

"I'm your death," she told it. Then she pounded at the image with the metal bar. As Zach said, it was indeed a hologram, just a collection of light beams. She couldn't physically hurt it, but the metal bar appeared to interfere with its electric current and light frequency. She swung repeatedly at the image until it roared, flickered, and vanished.

The dungeon vanished along with the creature. Mya and Zach were back in the middle of the exhibition. It was dark, closed up for the night. No one else was around. Zach lay on the floor, semi-conscious. Mya pulled out her phone to call emergency, and Zach groped in the dark for her hand. She held his hand tightly, and he relaxed.

"No doctor," he said and then passed out.

"That's great, Zach. You want no help, and now you're dead weight for me to carry," she griped as she called a cab.

She dragged him toward a wall and propped him up against it. While they waited for the cab, she checked her scorecard even though she knew she would not have earned this point. She may have saved Zach down in the dungeon, if it was indeed a real location, but his profile hadn't been flagged as being in immediate danger, so his saved life wouldn't count. Right now, however, she wasn't concerned about the point. She was just glad Zach was safe.

What had happened in the dungeon didn't seem to register on her scorecard at all. Mya was pondering that fact when she heard the sound of the car engine.

Zach stirred when he heard it. She asked the cab to take them to his apartment. She rolled her eyes to herself at the thought that yes, she had stalked him. She knew where he lived, and she knew he lived alone.

CHAPTER 12

Mya spent the night in Zach's apartment. She was worried about leaving him alone. During the night, she left her deity vision on so she could do her work. Dan's files confirmed that he was still alive. She logged his file as a case she was in charge of. If he died of unnatural causes, it would count against her record. But if she could save Dan in the next seven days, it would be one point up for her.

Her deity network must have given her incorrect information about the fire, and she understood the reason why. Her deity intelligence network was based on observation by the deity minions. They had no skills, no training, and no support. Their bland job description included staring at the world through blurry eyes and relating the information to her via their primitive technology. She speculated that they had gotten wind of the red painting and had thought it was a fire. After all, it *had* sucked Dan into it.

But what was the gateway Zach had referred to? How had her system and the Gods' files totally missed it? And how had they totally missed the incident down at the dungeon? If she hadn't gone down there with Zach, would he have been killed? She was in charge of his safety, so it should have come under her radar that he was in danger. But there hadn't been a whiff of information about the dungeon or the weird holograms.

A few weeks ago, Zach had suddenly disappeared. She had received no signal from her network. Mya remembered the day vividly as she had just returned from London after saving one of her subjects. She had looked for him everywhere. The only reason she hadn't pulled a gigantic multiversal search and rescue for Zach was because her file suggested that he was fine but had switched dimensions and gone to a place her jurisdiction couldn't reach.

Zach was different when he came back. She could no longer read his mind. The information had become sketchy, and he was sending out waves of a strange energy she had never before encountered. She didn't understand what he had done with the holograms. Why had the light waves in the dungeon affected him so much? Why didn't he want to go to the hospital? Why did he say it was his fault if something happened to Dan? There were so many questions she needed to ask him.

Mya looked at Zach, watching him sleep for a bit. Finally, she switched back to her human vision. In her human body, she was unbearably tired. She curled up on the sofa and willed herself to sleep.

Mya woke in the morning, refreshed. Zach was sitting on the chair opposite the sofa looking at her. Her eyebrows rose up as soon as she registered her surroundings and imagined her before-coffee-and-make-up morning look. She was facing Zach. He must have been watching her sleep. She had stayed up most of the night, so that meant she had to look pretty rough right now. Mya silently wondered if she snored.

Zach smiled and pushed a cup of black coffee in front of her. The coffee mug's contents were still steaming, suggesting he had just made it.

"Good morning." He smiled at her.

Mya sat up and grabbed the mug of coffee as if it were a rare diamond. She held it up to her face and inhaled the rich coffee aroma. The caffeine, along with a hint of bitter spice and a floral blend, surged through her system. She smiled as she recalled that Zach was a coffee snob.

"Good coffee." She smiled back at him over the rim of her coffee mug. "You want to ask me how I knew Dan was in trouble."

Zach nodded and leaned back in his chair.

"I'm kinda psychic."

He shook his head. "You're either psychic or you're not."

Mya wasn't sure that telling Zach that she was a deity was a good idea. She shrugged. "All right, I'm psychic. I can sense danger around people I know and care about. But it's not a gift. It's a curse. So I'd prefer not to discuss it. I know you have gifts you don't want to talk about, either. Like the way you saw the tunnel. The way you looked at the holographic girl and attacked her with your gaze."

Zach's eyes darkened, but he said nothing.

"So let's make a deal. You don't ask me about my unusual business, and I won't ask you about yours. Deal?"

Zach didn't answer the question.

"Deal or no deal, Zach?"

He looked straight into her eyes, and she felt a pang of guilt for not telling him the truth.

"I need your help," he said, "so how about this—I won't ask you about your secret business, but you *can* ask me. I'll tell you what I can. Then I need you to help me find Dan. Psychic or not, you can sense him, and I can't. I can't let anything happen to him. Not only because he's my best friend, but also because I need to take him to a place where he'll play a very important role. Many lives depend on this."

She stared at him. "That's low, Zach."

"Is that a yes?"

"I'll let you know after I get dressed." She stood and went into the bathroom.

***

When Mya entered the bathroom, she switched on her deity vision. She shuffled through the files in her mind.

"Oh no, no, no!" She wanted to pound her head against the wall. Zach's file had come up overnight after she had fallen asleep.

He had come back to Earth, and his profile was now flagged. But he wasn't on the file of those she should protect—he was on the list that was destined to die. This was top profile, and effectively, in earthly terms, his case was now beyond her pay scale. If she went out of her way to save him, the consequences would be unimaginable.

Was this Ishtar's ultimatum?

She just realized that the biggest mistake she had made in the last thousand years wasn't signing that contract with her Goddess without reading the fine print but allowing Zach, a human, to become too important to her.

CHAPTER 13

She switched off her deity mode, got dressed, and went out to the living room. Her body and her mind were numbed by the new information. She knew he was going to die, and she wasn't allowed to save him. Even if she decided to break the rules and save him, as she did all the time, she could never be certain that she was capable of doing so. Most of the time, individuals on the dead list were killed by forces much stronger than her minor deity power.

"I'm going with you," she said dryly and headed toward the door.

"Don't you want to know where we're going?"

"You can fill me in on the way."

"Yes, but—"

Mya raised an eyebrow.

Zach sighed. "I don't want you to feel obliged to go."

"You have to work a lot harder to make me do things I don't want to do, Zach. We should go before I change my mind." She turned on her heel and exited the room. Zach followed.

***

Zach zoomed along the highway on his motorbike like there was no tomorrow. Although Mya didn't have a problem with speed, her stomach nevertheless quivered. She tried to hang on to her organs to be sure they stayed where they belonged.

Zach's cell phone buzzed in his pocket.

"Do you want me to take the call?" Mya asked.

"Check the caller ID."

Mya pulled the phone out and checked. "It's Chloe," she said, feeling her stomach sink.

Chloe was Zach's childhood sweetheart. In terms of looks, she was flawless with a perfect oval face, full lips, striking eyes, sunny blonde hair, and a model-tall body. In terms of career, she was a successful fashion designer. And in terms of sentimental connection with Zach, well, according to her file, Zach had never been with another girl.

"Do you want to take the call?"

Zach shook his head. Mya let the call go to voice mail.

"She left a message. Do you want to listen?"

Zach shook his head again.

Mya heard the skidding sound of tires on the road, and at the same time, an engine roared. Zach heard it, too. On a side street, a small truck headed straight for them as if navigated by someone who had been lying in wait for them. The truck had already been speeding and had gained momentum before they reached the street.

Zach was calm as steel. He did not swerve the motorbike but accelerated. The truck missed them and continued to skid and fishtail across the road. Mya didn't have to look to know that the nasty sounds they left behind were accidents occurring like falling dominos, one after the other.

"Should we stop and check?" Mya asked.

Zach nodded. He made a U-turn and drove toward the crash site. It was chaos. The truck had hit a light pole, making it fall over. The pole had hit the front of a furniture shop. People had gotten out of their cars to check out the scene. A man standing next to an SUV was on the phone to emergency. The hood of a small Hyundai was squashed into the back of a minivan in front of it. With the hood pushed back and up, the Hyundai looked as if it was about to sneeze. The young female driver appeared unharmed and was on her phone as well.

Zach parked the motorbike and walked toward the truck. He could see no driver in the cab. He looked inside, and his face turned as white as a sheet. Mya darted over to take a look. Zach pulled at her elbow,

"Don't," he said. He tried to pull her away, but she shrugged off his grip and peeked in.

On the driver's seat was a puddle of black substance. In the puddle, wormlike creatures the size of small lizards swam and slithered around. The steamy stench in the cab nauseated Mya. She reeled away from the truck and didn't realize she was leaning into Zach's supporting arms. Zach took her to the side of the street. She pressed her palm against a light pole and willed herself not to vomit. After a while, she calmed down.

Zach held her shoulders and asked, "Are you all right now?"

She nodded.

"I'm sorry you saw that. I didn't expect them to bring it here. Nasty sons of bitches," Zach grumbled.

"What do you mean? Who are you talking about?"

"I—"

There was a *whoosh*, and a bullet hit Zach's shoulder, sending him staggering back a few steps. Then he dove, pulling Mya with him to the ground and covering her with his body. Another bullet hit the light pole next to where she had just stood.

CHAPTER 14

The fear he would die in front of her clawed at her heart. It wasn't a matter of how but when. If Ishtar wouldn't allow her to save Zach, it was cruel to make her watch him die.

Wait. Ishtar wasn't making her watch—she had chosen to be here. The reason she was with Zach was because it was the fastest way to save Dan. Ishtar only required her to save Dan, so that meant every action she took and every decision she made might change the sequence of events. She might be able to get Zach off the dead list without directly saving him.

Zach grabbed at his wound. Blood seeped out through the gaps between his fingers. He winced but looked more annoyed than in pain. "If that's the best you can do, I feel sorry for your asses," Zach muttered, looking off into the distance.

Mya followed his gaze. The shadows of four men darted into an empty loading zone on a back street. Zach clenched his teeth and tightened his jaw. "There are four of them, Zach, if you're going to do what you're thinking."

"Only four of them?" Zach winked at her then turned and charged toward the shadows.

Mya followed.

"Mya, you should stay here."

"What if more of them come while you're chasing those four?"

He looked around and nodded. "Okay, follow me, but stay behind me at all times. Can you do that?"

Mya nodded.

They approached an abandoned port. The shops at the front were no longer in operation, thus the back streets were deserted. It was dark. The walls were full of graffiti, some good and some bad like the tattoos you might get on a drunken night only to regret them the next day.

Zach pushed Mya into a corner between two large dumpsters. "Stay here. Don't move, no matter what happens."

He darted across an open space toward an industrial bin. Bullets rained after him. He caught another bullet but kept going. The four shadows followed Zach. He raced past two bins, and they shot at him again. Zach was hit once more. He slowed down and then sped up again, running across another exposed area. The four men came out of hiding and charged straight at him with their guns. They shot at him, and he fell to the floor and stayed down, sprawled on the ground, motionless.

The men approached him. When they were close, Zach sprung to his feet. He lifted his jacket and pulled out two golden daggers.

"Greetings from Eudaiz," he said and smirked.

With lightning speed, he swung the two daggers. Before the four men could blink, their body parts were scattered across the floor. The bodies quickly dissolved into black pools on the ground.

"If you want me dead, then send real soldiers," Zach muttered to himself. Then he tucked his daggers away and went for Mya. He found her where he'd left her. She leaned against the wall and stared at him.

"They weren't men, Mya. I didn't kill four men in front of you."

"I'm not shocked if that's what you're thinking."

"But you almost fainted before."

"I don't like worms."

Zach nodded. "Fair enough." Then he winced and shifted his left shoulder.

"You were shot," Mya panicked. "You were shot before, and now you have even more injuries."

Zach nodded. "Yeah, another one in the shoulder and two in my back. They aren't fatal. I'll be fine."

"You have four bullets in your body. We've got to get you to the hospital."

"I can't go to the hospital."

"You can't, or you won't?"

He shook his head.

"Any ordinary human would have done a face plant right now with four bullets in his body. What are you, Zach, if you're not a machine?"

"I'm still human, Mya."

She narrowed her eyes. "Still? You're either human or you're not."

"Let's just say I have a special power—some kind of energy. These bullets won't kill me. If we go back to my apartment and you take the bullets out, I'll be as good as new with a little rest. As I promised, I'll tell you more. But not now. We have to leave before more of them come."

Mya nodded. They headed back toward Zach's motorbike.

"You're not thinking of driving this, are you?" Mya spoke, eyeing the blood seeping from Zach's wounds.

"Huh?" Zach was a bit dazed from the blood loss.

Mya grabbed the helmet. "Can you hang on until we get to your apartment? I don't want you to fall onto the road."

"You—"

"Yes, I can drive a motorbike. Do you have a problem with that?"

A smile came across Zach's sinfully handsome but tired face. "No, on the contrary, if you can handle this beast, I can certainly hang on."

CHAPTER 15

In the apartment, Zach took off his jacket and his shirt and tossed them onto the table. Mya opened the first-aid box they had bought on the way back and fumbled with its contents as she tried to control her surge of hormones at the sight of a shirtless Zach.

"What will you need for the pain?" she asked.

Zach went to the kitchen and pulled a bottle of scotch from the cabinet above the kitchen bench.

"I'll need some of that, too," Mya said dryly, snatching the bottle out of Zach's hand and taking a swig.

Zach cocked an eyebrow.

She smiled and said, "Good stuff" then turned and went into the living room.

Zach followed her and settled on the sofa. He took a sip from the bottle.

"What's that?" Mya pointed at a red scar that looked like a thumbprint on Zach's inner right forearm, close to his elbow.

"It's a birthmark," he said.

"You ready?" Mya asked.

He nodded.

Mya started cutting into his flesh just deep enough to get the bullet out. She knew it had to hurt like hell, but Zach didn't even wince. He just continued to sip from the bottle.

"When you killed those things that turned into puddles of black sludge and worms, you said 'greetings from Eudaiz.' What's Eudaiz?"

There was a brief moment of hesitation, then Zach said, "It's the place where I live now."

She knew as soon as she heard him say it that it wasn't on Earth. She thought Zach must feel really odd talking about it. But nothing was weirder than her background.

She removed the bullets and cleaned the blood off of his back. As soon as he stood up, a knife flew in through the window and slashed his side. He pushed her aside into a corner of the room. A shadow darted through the window and rolled on the floor. A man stood up, and without a word, he attacked Zach.

Zach darted to the table where he had dropped his jacket and his daggers and grabbed the weapons. Zach and the man fought. Mya had had no idea Zach was so good in hand-to-hand combat. The man was obviously a professional, but after a few rounds, he started to lose ground to Zach. He ducked to the side, and the next thing Mya knew, he had dragged her out in front of him and had pressed a knife to her throat.

"Let her go," Zach growled.

"One slice of my knife, and I'll detach her head from her neck. Now put your daggers down. Take your wrist unit off and give it to me."

Zach didn't hesitate. He dropped the daggers and took the watch he was wearing off, throwing it toward the attacker. When the man was distracted by the watch, Mya swiveled, ducked, and elbowed him.

She twisted out of his grip and fled. But she made it only two steps before he grabbed her again. Zach interfered with a kick, but because of the tight space in the living room, they all struggled and stumbled into the broken furniture.

The man went for the weak link every time, and unfortunately, it was her. She fell to the floor. He gave Zach a kick, sending Zach backward, and then jumped toward her with his knife, stabbing at her in a downward motion.

She had seen and been involved in many ritual fights in the last thousand years and had many times been at the pointy end of a knife. If she switched to her deity mode right now, she might be able to get out of the situation as she'd done several hundred times before. But this time, she thought it might be too late.

He could have taken her out, but he had slowed his attack by a fraction of a second. He was intentionally giving Zach an opportunity to attack him.

She wanted to call out to Zach, but she was too slow.

Zach fell right into the man's trap and tried to grab him from behind.

The assailant immediately swiveled around, turned the knife toward Zach, and slashed through his birthmark. Zach staggered back, clutching his wound. The four bullets hadn't done much damage, but this simple cut left him speechless. He slumped to his knees, and the blood drained from his face.

The man smirked. He was so confident that Zach wouldn't be able to move that he turned his back on him to look at Mya. "Mya Portman, congratulations! You tried to save someone you shouldn't have, and now you're about to lose him. Your boss won't be happy about this. Let me finish him for you."

She roared. "I didn't try to save him. But I will now." She no longer cared what she should or shouldn't do.

Her deity mode was on instantly. Her second best skill as a deity was her hand-to-hand combat technique—she sometimes referred to it as scuffling. She was a hell of a fighter—the best in court in her time. Ishtar would never house anyone without a talent.

Mya twirled around, and in a short moment, before the man could blink, she had thrown him to the floor so hard she heard his bones crack. Then she pulled him up to his feet and pressed him against the wall. She grabbed his knife and pointed it between his eyes. The man closed his eyes, waiting for the blade to penetrate his skull.

She stopped.

More than a thousand years on duty, and she had never killed an unarmed and defeated man. She released him.

"What's your name?"

"Lucas Hine. Thank you for letting me go."

"Don't thank me too soon. There won't be a next time. Drop the watch and go."

Lucas nodded, dropped the watch to the floor, and fled the scene immediately. She wanted to question him more, but she had Zach to tend to. He was her priority.

Zach lay on the ground in silence. What ran out from the gash on his arm wasn't blood but a semi-transparent silvery substance. Whatever it was, losing it was weakening him by the second. She rushed over, grabbed the medical box, and rummaged through it for bandages.

"My wrist unit." Zach's voice was barely audible, but she heard him. She scrambled to the center of the room where Lucas had dropped the watch and brought it back to Zach. When she placed it into his hand, he pressed his thumb onto the screen. Something seemed to activate on the device.

"Ayana," Zach whispered, propping himself up on his elbows.

"Do you need to sit up?" She touched his shoulder, trying to help him sit up.

"Leave me here, Mya…"

"No."

"Leave now…"

"Hell no."

A beam of light appeared in the middle of the room, coming from above like a spotlight on a stage. Zach flopped to the floor on his back, totally out of it. The light moved in their direction. She could feel the vibration of energy from it. The floor shook.

She leaned over and lay on top of Zach, covering him as much as she could, and waited for something to happen.

CHAPTER 16

Dan scrambled to his feet after a guard threw him into a dark cell like he was a rag doll. He hated being handled. He had been on his phone at the art exhibition center when he saw Zach and Mya running toward him. He was being extra cautious after the fire the day before. Someone or something was setting traps for Zach, and he knew it.

It wasn't the first time they'd been attacked. Zach was not only a magnet for his female fans, but he also attracted supernatural disasters. The difference between the two of them was that Dan believed in and understood supernatural forces, and Zach didn't.

Zach had disappeared a few weeks ago. He often did that when he got an inspiration for his music. Then yesterday someone wanted to burn him to lure Zach into a trap. But a trap for what?

Dan punched the wall but figured that, apart from hurting his knuckles, the action wasn't going to get him out of the cell. He began to pace around the cell and think.

***

The light beam grew wide and spun harder. Mya could feel the searing heat against her skin. Loose objects in the room were swept from where they rested and sent crashing to the floor. Then the heat subsided, and Mya felt a warm sensation blanket her body. She was lying on top of Zach, face down. She could see a rim of bright light around her. The energy was still vibrating. She wanted to look up, but she didn't want to leave Zach. The light was merely warm on her body, but she wasn't sure what effect it might have on him. She remembered that when they had been in the dungeon, the electric current had had no impact on her, but it had almost killed him.

For a while, nothing happened. She turned her head to the side and glanced up. In the middle of the light beam, she saw a hologram of a beautiful woman. She had long white hair and striking blue eyes and wore a long white gown.

She smiled at Mya. "Zach called for me. I'm here to help if you'll let me take a look at him."

"What's your name?"

"Ayana."

Mya recalled Zach calling out that name. She must be telling the truth. She rolled off of Zach.

Serenely, the woman called Ayana walked out from the circle of light. Mya could feel her presence and the heat emitting from her body. She was sure the woman had just then turned from a hologram into a being with a solid body.

The circle of light enlarged further, washing over Zach and Mya. She felt a warm current rush over her body and realized she was now inside the circle.

Ayana kneeled down next to Zach. She pulled out a black wristband and snapped it on his right wrist. Within a few seconds, Zach stirred, opened his eyes. He was groggy at first, and he lay still on the floor, staring up at the ceiling. Shortly, he registered what had just happened. He bolted up and grabbed Mya's arms, looking up and down her body.

"Are you okay?" he asked.

"I'm fine. But I should be asking you that question, Zach."

Ayana cast a warm glance at Mya. "What are you, beautiful girl?" Ayana asked.

"Thank you for calling me beautiful. But I'm not sure how I should take the fact that you consider me a *what* instead of a *who*."

Ayana smiled. "Humans can't handle the gate the way you do."

"What gate?" Mya asked, raising an eyebrow.

Zach growled, "You could have killed her, Ayana. How am I supposed to live with that?"

"You asked her, and she didn't leave you, Zach."

"Then you shouldn't have come out of the teleport!" Zach exclaimed.

"It might have cost her life, but I had to save you."

"I'd rather die than—"

"Be mindful, Zach," Ayana cut in, her eyes darkening, "Think carefully before you finish that sentence. You are responsible for more than just your own life."

"Don't try to manipulate me. I won't do this if it costs a single soul. And especially not hers." Zach pointed at Mya.

"If you don't want to be in such a position, then you shouldn't be reckless in your actions. Her life is the same as others. Any war costs lives, Zach," Ayana snarled.

"Hey!" Mya waved her arm without success to get some attention.

"Her life isn't like others. No harm will come to my friends and family. You promised me that.

Now Dan is missing, the Xiilok soldiers beat us here, and you're saying I'm reckless." Zach kept his voice down, but Mya could hear the anger boiling in it.

"Are you sure?" Ayana frowned.

"Xiilok!" Mya couldn't stop the word from coming out of her mouth. Xiilok was the universe of the multiversal outlaws. No one could touch that universe, including her Goddess. Zach and Ayana looked at her. She shrugged. "I just wanted to get your attention. Dan might be okay right now, but someone has to save him or he'll be dead soon. If you two are too busy bickering, I'll have to save him myself."

Mya turned on her heel and walked straight into the wall of light surrounding her. She hit the wall so hard that she bounced back a few steps and saw stars. She was still standing in the light circle and couldn't walk through it even though it looked transparent.

"Ouch." She rubbed her forehead. Then she whirled around and snarled at Ayana, "Let me go."

"How do you know Dan isn't dead?" Ayana asked.

"She's a psychic," Zach responded.

"I can speak for myself," Mya protested.

Ayana looked at Zach. "Are you sure about the soldiers?"

He nodded. "They sent Xiilok fighters. I saw them."

The color drained out of Ayana's face, "You can't fight them on your own. I'll have to consult the council and get back to you. But before then, take no action. You know how many lives we're responsible for. If you fail, all of those souls will be lost. Don't be reckless, Zach."

Ayana nodded a goodbye to Mya. With a gracious whirl, she disappeared as smoothly as she had come. The light circle disappeared with her.

CHAPTER 17

The room returned to its normal lighting and temperature. Zach approached Mya and gently lifted her chin to check the bruise on her forehead. His green eyes locked intensely on the faint mark as if he could wipe it away using his willpower.

"Are you some kind of warrior from another planet?" Mya asked.

"What does your psychic mind tell you?"

"I can't read your mind."

"Are you sure about Dan being okay?"

She nodded. Her deity mode was still on, and she had just checked. Dan was fine. She was waiting for the next signal from her network of his whereabouts. "Yes, I'm sure he's okay. I have my sources, and they told me he's alive. They'll let me know of his location soon. My sources have supernatural power if that makes you feel any more confident."

Zach nodded. "Do you have supernatural power, too?"

She shook her head. "I can't tell you. At least for now because I'm unsure of the consequences."

Zach gazed at her for a short moment, then he smiled. "I'm not a warrior of any kind. But I have the ability to send a sort of sound wave into people's heads. For the most part, I've just used it to annoy people since I was a kid. But in a universe that's far from here, they recognized my ability as a talent. That universe is called Eudaiz." He paused there and said, "How am I doing?"

Mya nodded. "So far, so good."

"Eudaiz is governed by a council of nine, including eight councillors and a king. The councillors, or Sciphils in their terms, govern their own districts. Ayana Dee, the woman you just saw, is Sciphil Two. She recruited me as her successor a few months ago. As a successor, my body was transformed. I can heal quickly from ordinary wounds. But I'm not invincible. My body is very sensitive to extraterrestrial frequencies."

"The currents that hit you in the dungeon?"

He nodded. "And I have only a limited amount of the special energy—that's the silver substance you saw leaking out from my gash earlier." Zach looked at Mya, gauging his progress.

She nodded. "And I'm guessing your energy is rechargeable. That's what Ayana just did."

Zach chuckled. "Not exactly, but close. They call it healing. And it can only be done in Eudaiz. What Ayana gave me was a quick fix so that I can get back there."

She narrowed her eyes. "So if you're injured again before you go back..."

He shook his head. "I'll try my best to avoid that. This isn't a birthmark. It's a seal where the energy was originally injected into me." He pointed to the mark on his right arm and grinned.

She nodded. "Ayana said you're in charge of a lot of people. How many people, exactly?"

"The last record showed our district accommodates more than ninety-five billion."

So much for counting my scorecard trying to make it to a thousand, she thought.

"There's a district in need of a councillor, and Dan is designated for the position."

"Does he know this? Did he agree to it? He didn't sound like he knew."

Zach shook his head and smiled. "I'll talk to him. I know him. He'll agree. But the job isn't easy. Eudaiz is at war, so it's dangerous. After we get Dan, and I take him back to Eudaiz, I wish you wouldn't get any further involved in this mess. You see, I couldn't protect you before."

"You don't get to tell me what to do, Zach. I come and go as I please. And because I didn't do what you wanted me to do, I saved your ass in the dungeon. You might think you're a superhero, but do you really think you could have driven home after the gunfight with four bullets in your body? And did you think I was going to leave you to bleed your silver blood out all over the pavement while—"

Zach locked his lips on hers, stopping the flow of her eloquent speech. Then he pushed her against the wall and knocked the mighty deity breath out of her. His kiss was meant to conquer and possess. There was no nipping, testing, or gradual attempt at penetration. He asked for no permission.

His hands slid beneath her shirt, searching for her skin. His fingers pressed against her sensitive nerves, causing her system to explode wildly beyond what a thousand years' worth of being a deity could contain. He pressed his body against hers so hard that she could feel every muscle in his body quivering.

She reached her arms around him, and he hitched her hips up so that she could wrap her long legs around his waist. She received, she responded, and she was ready to give back.

Then suddenly, he eased away from her and put her back down on the floor. Kissing her cheek and stepping back, he left her leaning against the wall, panting and gasping for breath. Her lips were swollen, and her eyes watered.

"I'm sorry. I'm a jerk."

"For what you just did, yes you are."

His phone buzzed on the table, and he absently snatched it up and answered it, his eyes still locked with Mya's.

"Yeah."

Zach snapped back to reality when he heard Chloe's voice on the phone. "Chloe," he muttered and sat down on the sofa.

Mya rolled her eyes. She knew she was no competition for Chloe. She shouldn't be in a relationship anyway. She was a good deity, and she had a job to do. It was her duty to protect Zach, and she should have kept the relationship at an acquaintance level.

She tidied her shirt and grabbed her bag.

"Yes, a couple of days," Zach said on the phone as his eyes followed Mya.

She went to the bathroom to collect her belongings. She had only stayed here one night, but she could see her marks already—some hair on the floor, a splotch of her night cream on the vanity bench, the faint sense of her perfume. She cleaned up as much as she could and went back to the living room.

"No, Chloe. We talked about this. You have to move on."

Mya nodded a goodbye to Zach and headed toward the door.

"Yes, that was part of the reason." He still talked on the phone, but he raced toward the door before Mya got there to block her way out. Mya stared at him, appalled at his nerve.

"Chloe, if you don't move on, I will... I'm seeing someone else." Zach stared back at Mya.

Mya walked around him to get to the door. He grabbed her elbow.

"That would be best. Bye, Chloe."

Zach pulled Mya back into the apartment and slammed the door shut. She glared at him. He stared back.

"What do you want, Zach?"

"Don't you have to slap me in the face first?"

"That's what ordinary girls do. I'm not ordinary." She stared into his eyes and saw pain. "Let me go, Zach. This isn't going to work." Her throat burned as she said it. She sidestepped Zach to get to the door. He grabbed her arms.

"I know you're not an ordinary girl. I've spilled my secrets to you. Now it's your turn."

"I didn't promise to tell you anything."

"You promised to help me get Dan back."

She paused. *He's right*. He nudged her back inside and pushed her backward, sitting her down on the sofa.

He sat down on the coffee table and held her hands, more to ensure she couldn't bolt for the door than as any kind of sentimental gesture.

"I don't want you to think I'm fooling around with you and Chloe. A few weeks ago, I broke up with her before I took a trip that I had no clue if I would return from. She heard I was back, so she called."

"If your trip was the reason you broke up with her, then she has every right to contact you now that you're back."

Zach shook his head. "I'm not back for good, Mya. I have to take Dan to Eudaiz. And that universe is at war."

"So you're asking him to go there to die. And you'll go back there to die, too?"

He shook his head. "No. We'll win this war. But as in any battle, there will be sacrifices. If the sacrifice is my life, so be it."

"You'd die for strangers?"

"You can't fight a battle on that scale with such a mentality, Mya. I took on that responsibility, and I will follow through with it. There are millions of people and families who rely on me to make it back to Eudaiz with Dan. They expect us to protect them because we are their councillors. I don't expect you to understand."

"Why? Because I'm a woman who might need protection?"

He gazed deeply into her eyes. She had known him forever, but he had hardly had a chance to know her. She raised an eyebrow in challenge and met his gaze.

"I did something in the past that I'm not proud of, Mya. For years, I lived in guilt, and in those dark years, Chloe was always there for me. I didn't rely on her for emotional comfort. But she was too innocent to bear a broken heart. So I let it slide. I let the boundary between us blur. And that was a mistake."

She nodded.

"When Ayana offered me a chance to go to Eudaiz to serve a greater cause, I took it. The trip was dangerous, and I thought I would never come back, so I broke up with her before that."

"When did I come in?"

He smiled. "You didn't just come into to my life. You stormed in and robbed me of my heart. And don't worry, I'm not going to write a song about it."

He held her hands and looked into her eyes. "The night you walked into my club, I knew I was in trouble. Something about you brought out the beast in me. I desired you. I couldn't get you out of my head. But I'd promised Ayana to go to Eudaiz, so I did my best to keep my distance from you. But every ounce of my body hurt just thinking about it."

"Now that you've told me, what will you do next?"

He grabbed his jacket and stood up.

"I just want you to know that I'm not fooling around with you. Our king in Eudaiz is going through the coronation process, and it's more dangerous than ever. I don't want you to get involved in any way." He strode toward the door.

She talked to his back. "You think you might die during this fight, and you're willing to accept that?"

He turned. "Great victory has a price, Mya. If the price for Eudaiz's peace is my life, then it's a bargain. But trust me, I'll try my best not to die."

"Don't you want me to help you find Dan anymore?" she asked as he walked toward the door.

He smiled at her. "I can handle this. Stay here and be safe." Then he walked away.

She didn't realize it, but a tear had rolled down her face.

CHAPTER 18

Zach parked his motorbike at the corner of a back street. He checked his wrist unit again and saw that the confirmation of Dan's location had been sent to him. He had asked for help from his friend in the Daimon Gate, and this information was from a wicked multiversal spy system called the EYE. Normally, he wouldn't ask because retrieving information across dimensions was not only illegal but also dangerous. But he needed the information. Zach didn't have many close friends, but in situations like this, his few friendships always worked out for the best.

Zach hid a distance away behind a light pole that faced the building. It was an abandoned industrial area where endless blocks of warehouses provided a haven for criminal activities. The building where Dan was being held was a large, rusty wool store.

He didn't know exactly where the room or cell where they held Dan was, nor did he know how many goons were inside the building. He needed to rescue Dan, and he needed to do it fast. If he failed to take him back to Eudaiz at the designated time, millions of lives would be lost. He didn't want that weighing on his shoulders.

The front door opened, and Lucas came out. Once he had left the building, Zach made his way to the warehouse. He tried the door and was surprised to find it unlocked. He slipped inside, crouched low, and looked around.

There was a staircase to his right leading up and a long hallway off to his left. Zach doubted they'd be keeping a prisoner upstairs, so he started down the long hall to his left. He kept going until the hallway ended at another staircase. This one went down to another closed door.

Taking out his daggers, he descended the stairs slowly, wincing each time one creaked. Finally reaching the door, he turned the knob and pushed it open. The door opened up into a large cement chamber. It looked empty from where Zach stood, but he knew it could just be another illusion. He stepped in cautiously, and within seconds, he was surrounded by at least eight of Lucas's men.

They were Xiilok soldiers, Zach was sure of it. Xiilok was a land of no return for ordinary humans and creatures. When creatures joined Xiilok, they turned into entities invisible to technology in any other universe. When they died, they melted into puddles of worms. Zach had heard of Xiilok, but he had never been to Xiilok before, nor did he have any intention of doing so.

Zach took on a fighting stance, his daggers at the ready. One of the soldiers came at him with his sword drawn. Zach brandished his daggers, and they circled each other. The other guards watched as if amused that Zach would even try to fight. He and the guard crossed sword and dagger. The sword was longer, but the dagger was thicker and in spite of his injuries and the size of his opponent, Zach was stronger. After a desperate struggle, Zach was able to knock the guard's sword from his hand, and it went sailing across the room. Then, surprising the others, Zach threw a roundhouse kick and knocked a guard who was sneaking up on him from behind against the far wall. That was when the guards realized what they were up against and came at him full force.

Zach put up a desperate fight, seriously injuring several of the guards and mortally wounding another. The others stared in shock at the puddle of remains their colleague had become before charging him all at once and taking him down to the floor. Zach dropped the daggers and raised his hands over his head in surrender.

Although he couldn't understand their words, he could tell by their chatter that they were trying to decide among themselves what to do with him. Zach hoped he was right and that Lucas would have told them to take him alive. After several agonizing minutes of armed barbarians discussing his fate in a foreign tongue, Zach was hauled roughly to his feet and propelled forward through the cold cement tunnel.

One of the barbarians unlocked a cold, dank cell and another of them literally threw him in. His body hit the cement wall and then fell to the floor. Zach lay still and pretended to be unconscious until they left.

Then he heard Dan's voice. "Zach, oh God, are you okay? Answer me!" He felt Dan's hands shake his shoulders.

He opened one eye and then the other, looked at Dan, and grinned.

"Jesus Christ, you prick!" Dan exclaimed.

Zach dragged his bruised, battered, and bloody body to a sitting position. "I'm really hurt!"

Dan exhaled. "At least you aren't dead. Why did you let them haul your ass in here?"

"Because it was the quickest way to find you and haul *your* ass out of here. Did you talk to the guy who grabbed you? Do you know what they want from you?"

Dan snorted. "Yeah, they asked me where I buried King Solomon's treasure. And I told them I left a hint in a temple on top of a mountain in Tibet."

Zach scowled.

Dan grinned. "Okay, not funny. No, they didn't talk to me. I think there's one badass and his girlfriend. The girl called him Lucas. The others are minions. They don't talk much. And they look weird."

Zach shook his head. "As a matter of fact, they don't talk at all."

"Even robots talk."

"As you said, they're minions. But no need to worry about them. Did you get anything from Lucas's girlfriend?"

Dan grinned. "Indeed, I did. She had a weird accent, and she thought I was American."

"That's helpful!"

"Here's the juicy bit. She spoke on her cell phone, negotiating the money they could get if they arranged for us to be killed under a girl's watch. She also asked if whoever hired her wants her to kill the girl as well and whether they would get paid more for that. She yakked in French, thinking I wouldn't understand. She didn't mention the name of the girl, but she..." Dan trailed off as if he had realized something. And then the blood drained out of Zach's face.

"We're just pawns. They want Mya!" Zach muttered.

CHAPTER 19

Mya charged into the Babylonian court. She went first to Leon's chamber. She knocked several times without a response, so she let herself in. Leon wasn't there. She sat down on his bed and again and closed her eyes. She concentrated on Leon and only on him. That was when she saw him lying on a wooden slab in one of the courts very small confinement chambers.

Mya left the room and made her way down the long golden corridor. She wore her running shoes, so her feet made no sound. She'd left her Earth clothes on—she was on a mission and wasn't here to be seen in court in a gold bikini. She made her way around behind the huge gold throne on which her

Goddess sat when she held court and zigzagged around the large marble statues of the other Gods that ruled the land. Behind them were the confinement chambers where the offending citizens of Babylon were held while Ishtar decided their fate. Many of them ended their lives in the public arena with their heads rolling among the raucous spectators.

Mya walked until she came to the chamber where Leon lay. He jumped up and came to the barred slat in the door when he saw her.

"What are you doing here?"

"I need your help."

Leon held his arms out and said, "I'm not really in a position to help at the moment."

"Why are you locked up?" she asked him.

Leon looked down at the floor and then back up at her before saying, "That's not important, but the Goddess will be very unhappy if she finds you here. You have points to make up on your scorecard."

"Yes, I know. You told me already," Mya asked. "But you haven't answered my question. Why are you locked up? You spoke out about me, and that upset her, right? I thought Ishtar promoted you."

"What?"

"That's what you told me when you came to see me on Earth."

"No, I didn't. It's true you have two points to make it to zero. You're in the negative. When Ishtar mentioned the number and wanted to impose a deadline on you, I objected, and she threw me in here. But I never had a chance to tell you."

Mya braced her hands on the wall and tried to keep calm. *So who appeared to her in Zach's apartment using Leon's form?* She looked at Leon and knew he wouldn't last long here. "I'm going to beg for your pardon."

"No, Mya! That will just make her angrier—or worse, she'll want blood from you in return."

"You're here because you spoke for me. I'm not going to just leave you here. Besides, Zach is on the restricted list to die. And you know I'm not allowed to save subjects on that list. I need you to save him."

Leon snorted and raised his shackled hands.

"Trust me. I have a deal to make, and Ishtar is going to like it." Then she turned and walked away.

***

In the cell, Dan paced back and forth. "You're saying they're using us as bait to get Mya?"

Zach nodded. "Not get her, but get *to* her. Someone wants her to fail whatever the mission she is on. She mentioned before that it's her duty to protect us. She didn't explain further. But I get the impression that someone is trying to fail her by killing us under her watch."

"Is she some kind of FBI or CIA agent?"

Zach shook his head.

"MI5? MI6?"

"No. It has to do with something supernatural, Dan. I know you'll like this explanation much better than one that says she's a spy. She admitted she has supernatural power. But she wouldn't explain further."

"They want to bait her. So what do you want to do?"

Zach smiled. "We'll help them!"

***

Mya stood in front of Ishtar's chamber and took three deep breaths before she knocked. The door was opened by her servant, Elyse. Elyse had been with Ishtar for over a hundred years now, so she knew Mya on sight.

"Mya! Were we expecting you?"

"No, Elyse, but it's urgent that I speak to our Goddess. Is she available now?"

Elyse looked over her shoulder. Her Goddess was embroiled in a passionate romp with her latest lover behind the sheer curtains of her large bed.

"Not exactly, Mya. You can wait in the court, and I'll ask her if she can hear you today as soon as she...um...becomes available."

"Let her in. I'll see her," came Ishtar's grumpy voice from the bed chamber.

"Kneel at the altar. Your Goddess is about to arrive."

Mya didn't wait for a second invitation—she pushed her way in and kneeled next to the altar, waiting. In a short moment, she heard the sashay of Ishtar's robes and the jangle of the gold that dangled from her bronzed body.

Ishtar made her sweat it out for several minutes before saying, "Rise, Mya. What is so urgent that you disturb my pleasant afternoon off?"

"My Goddess, although I am unworthy, I'm here to ask a favor of you."

"A favor?" Ishtar said, raising one perfectly shaped eyebrow over her perfectly made-up golden brown eye.

"Yes, my Goddess, a favor. I am trying to save two of my subjects from certain death."

"Of course. That has been your one and only mission for more than a thousand years on Earth. But why do you have to ask for a favor from me?"

"My Goddess, one of the subjects has recently been switched to a restricted dead list. He's an important person from another universe. I should save him, Ishtar. I mean, *we* should save him."

"You think I should set aside important matters in court to take my time to swap around subjects on your list?"

"No, Ishtar. I understand that subjects are placed on lists due to several reasons that are beyond the court. But Zach Flynn is a subject with a great connection to a universe that we might want to build a good relationship with. So I ask that you not only give me permission to save him but also send help my way. Please send me Leon."

Ishtar raised both of her eyebrows, leaned back in the chair, and tapped her fingers on the golden armrests.

Mya cursed silently. This might be an overplay, and her head might be rolling on the floor soon.

"Which universe?"

"It's Eudaiz, Ishtar."

Ishtar shook her head. "There is no immediate benefit to us in dealing with Eudaiz."

"The connection with Eudaiz and killing Zach has to have something to do with us, my Goddess. Please give this some consideration. If it's not important, why would someone send a spy into the court and send a creature in Leon's form to make me rush around to save Zach only to fail because they sent Xiilok soldiers to kill him under my watch? Why would someone want me to make a mistake and fail?"

"Say that again," Ishtar's voice deepened. Mya grinned from ear to ear on the inside. She knew which button to press now. "I said someone wanted me to fail..."

"No, not that part. You mentioned Xiilok soldiers. Are you sure?"

"Oh, Xiilok. Yes, Ishtar, I'm certain. These creatures turned into worm puddles when they died."

Ishtar sat right up, narrowed her eyes.

"You can kill Xiilok soldiers?"

"No, Ishtar. I didn't kill them. Zach did."

"I see. And Zach is from Eudaiz. And he's on the dead list with Xiilok soldiers trying to kill him and you wanting to save him. So they'll kill him anyway. If you don't have my blessing, and you try to save a subject on the dead list, you'll be exiled. You'll be released from my protection and up for grab by any creature in any universe. If I give you the permission to save that subject, then I violate our own agreement and tarnish my reputation."

Mya looked at Ishtar. "You are the wisest Goddess of all time. These plots would never stop you from doing what you want."

Ishtar smiled. "And you are a smart little deity. You have my permission to save the subject. Not only that, I will send Leon to help you and make sure you succeed."

"Thank you, Ishtar. Please accept my utmost gratitude."

"Too soon. I will have to change your assignment. A new contract will be made for you. Once you've saved your subjects, you will come back to the court and take on the position of a minor deity of virginity."

Now Mya's head started to spin. A minor deity of virginity position would mean she would have to stay a virgin for all eternity. That would mean she and Zach could never—

"I accept," Mya heard her own voice say. Her brain hadn't quite caught up with her speech, and it surprised her. When her brain did finally catch up, she knew it was the only choice. If she refused, she'd be sacrificing Leon, Dan, and Zach. There was no way she could do that.

"Very well," Ishtar said and waved her hand absently in dismissal. In a short moment, she used the pen Elyse offered her, already dipped in golden ink, to signed the bottom of the scroll.

CHAPTER 20

Zach wagered the noise he and Dan were making was loud enough to capture the attention of the goons guarding the door. From the small window on the cell door, it would look like he was strangling Dan.

A couple of the guards stormed in. Before they could pull Zach and Dan apart, Zach had knocked one unconscious and disarmed the other.

Hearing the commotion, three more goons charged into the cell. Zach grinned as he grabbed one guard, bringing him down before he even knew what was happening. As he fell, his head slammed against the wall behind him, and Zach rammed his fist into the other guard's face.

While the two guards were stunned and blinded, Zach groped for one of the knives he knew they all carried. He stood up and drove the blade into the chest of the last standing goon. Their bodies disintegrated into brackish worm puddles.

Zach glanced at Dan, who stood in a corner, his back pressed against the wall.

Dan was a nerd and had never fought, not even for a parking spot. It wasn't that he was a coward. He opposed violence and refused to get involved in a fight unless it was absolutely necessary. Because Zach seemed quite capable of handling the fight by himself, Dan thought it best to stand back.

Zach snaked his hand into the pocket of a guard who looked like the one in charge and pulled out a big ring of keys. He was used to the electronic locks and automatic security system in Eudaiz, so this classic type of security amused him.

Zach and Dan raced out of the cell and had time for only a half second of celebration before the door at the end of the hall opened and Lucas came in with a group of Xiilok soldiers.

"Oh, crap!" Dan muttered. "You said yesterday that you wanted to take me to a place where I would play a very important role. Maybe that universe can send you some help? We could use a bit more manpower."

"In a normal situation, yes, Eudaiz can send soldiers to help us. But I told you they're at war, and my little mission here is considered trivial. We don't really have to fight these soldiers. I can open the teleport, and we can go right now."

Dan clenched his teeth. "Why didn't you do that in the cell before all the fighting and killing?"

Zach looked at Dan. "Because of Mya. I have to make sure we don't leave her behind to deal with the mess we created. Someone is using us to get her. And I think that person is using her to get to something even more important to the multiverse. This mission is not just about me grabbing you and teleporting back to Eudaiz as I originally thought. Someone is playing big games with the multiverse. We have to make sure he doesn't have the upper hand. We don't want to be his trump card."

Dan and Zach ran back, retreating into the cell from which they had just escaped.

"You better make sure your teleport works and that the roles we're going to take in Eudaiz pay well."

Zach rolled his eyes. "Bloody accountant."

***

Mya led Leon and a group of soldiers to the industrial area where her network had reported sightings of Zach and Dan. It took longer than she had thought to get help from the court. Apparently, because she and Leon had transported back and forth several times, it had grown easy for them. But for the soldiers who had never been to Earth, it was a hell of a trip via the dimensional channel.

It might be fair to make their travel difficult. If it was too easy to transport soldiers in large numbers between worlds and dimensions, universes would invade one another too often. Prosperous universes would be under constant threat of invasion.

The area was large, and she didn't like the feel of it. She switched on her deity vision and could see Zach and Dan stuck in a small cell at the far end. They were surrounded by Xillok fighters led by Lucas.

Mya gave careful instructions to Leon so that he could then give his soldiers some strategies.

"Be careful, Leon. You're excellent in hand-to-hand combat. But don't underestimate the weapons on Earth. Humans are experts at inventing weapons to kill one another. I don't know the impact guns will have on you and our soldiers. The Xiilok soldiers don't use guns, but Lucas, the professional human killer, does."

"Promise me you'll stay in your deity form the whole time," Leon said.

Mya nodded. "I need it. So yes."

The lined up in their planned strategic position and charged into the building.

CHAPTER 21

In the warehouse, Xiilok soldiers began to yell in loud, screechy voices. They approached the cell at the far end of the corridor. Mya had used her deity vision and had seen Zach and Dan in that cell. Sensing something unusual, Lucas turned around and saw her, Leon, and the Babylonian soldiers.

Lucas brought his little army to a halt. He could continue to advance his army and take out Zach and Dan, or he could turn and fight Mya and her people who were charging up behind him and would likely slaughter his army in return. He wasn't a Xiilok, and he had no supernatural power. He thought fighting humans like Dan and Zach would be his best bet. Lucas signaled the Xiilok fighters to charge at Mya and her people, and Lucas himself approached the cell.

He was sure Dan was just an ordinary accountant—a human he could kill with a flick of his fingers. But he didn't know Zach. Zach might have some supernatural power. But the tip he had gotten from his client which told him about the birthmark being Zach's fatal weak point seemed to help a lot. He might use that trick again this time.

The two groups of enemies faced one another. Leon, a tried and true battle hero, led his soldiers to the fight.

From a distance, Mya watched as Lucas turned around and approached the cell with a gun in one hand and a knife in the other. She saw Zach dart outside the cell. Seeing the gun, he pushed Dan back inside and slammed the door shut. He locked it from the outside, ignoring Dan's cursing. Then he turned to Lucas.

Saying nothing further, Mya charged toward the cell to rescue Dan. Zach fought Lucas away from the cell door. A shadow jumped out and stopped her on her way—it was a tall woman. There was something in the woman's eyes that made Mya uneasy.

"I don't need you here, Alice. Go away!" Lucas shouted at the woman while keeping his eyes locked with Zach.

The woman smiled at Mya. At the same time Lucas attacked Zach, the woman flew at Mya.

The woman was stronger than Mya had thought. Mya had her deity power on, but she could tell that the woman was no ordinary human. As for what kind of creature she was, Mya wasn't sure. The only thing she was sure about at the moment was that the woman was trying to stall her, not kill her. She was trying to prevent Mya from saving Dan, but she left open a view of the pathway to where Zach and Lucas were fighting so that Mya could see.

The woman either wanted her to see Zach die in front of her or wanted her to jump in to save Zach.

When Mya neither charged toward Dan's cell or ran toward Zach, the woman turned more vicious. From the corner of her eye, Mya could see that Leon had nearly reached the Xillok soldiers. Alice saw it, too. She flew at Mya. Her roar was deep and demonic. When her body was not in view of anyone but Mya, her hand turned into a blade, and she slashed at Mya.

Taken off guard, Mya staggered back, grabbing at the gash on her arm.

Zach saw it happen, and in the moment of losing his concentration, Lucas kicked him backward and followed with a jab of his knife. Zach blocked him, but when the knife got closer to Zach's body, Lucas flicked it up, deliberately slashing at the seal on Zach's arm.

Everything happened as if in slow motion in front of Mya. With all of her deity power, she shoved the woman to the wall so hard she almost passed out. Mya ran toward Zach, who had slumped to his knee, clutching his fatal wound.

Lucas stepped out in her way. With her momentum, she needed only to turn the dagger and she would have stabbed him in the heart. But she shoved him away instead.

She charged toward Zach as he fell into her arms. She held him. "Zach, please don't die!" she cried. He had told her if he was injured again, it would be fatal. It had happened too fast, in a blur of motion. And now he was going to leave forever.

"I won't die," Zach whispered into her ear as she held him.

She lowered him to the ground and looked into his tired face. She wiped a blood smear off it. "Tell me what to do, Zach." Tears streamed down her face.

"Take me back to Eudaiz."

"Can I?"

"Will you?"

"Yes, of course. If I can," she cried out.

"Not a chance," a demonic voice croaked from behind her.

Mya turned around and saw a shadow fly at her. She held up her dagger to block, and the blade pierced through Lucas's body.

Alice approached with a smirk on her face. She had thrown Lucas toward the tip of Mya's knife. The voice that came out of Alice's mouth wasn't human now. "Mya Portman, you've killed a human to save a subject on a dead list that isn't yours to save. You're now excluded from the protection of your Goddess. Your soul belongs to me."

"You killed your lover just to get me? How can you live with yourself for eternity?"

The woman laughed. "I'm not his little girlfriend. Alice thought she was in the wonderland for money and power. She was greedy. She annoyed my God. So I used her as my breakfast yesterday."

"You're wrong. I have permission to save Zach. I'm not violating any of my Goddess's rules."

The woman's face started to turn red. "I don't care. I have to have you." She shrieked out a stream of strange demonic sounds. Mya's body was numb. She couldn't move. It was as if the woman had put a spell on her. She wriggled and twisted, but nothing worked.

Leon had finished with the Xiilok creatures. He saw what was happening. He charged toward Mya.

The woman had grown to about ten feet tall. Her arms and legs stretched out, and her face distorted. She turned into a space creature, half ape and half lizard.

She flicked her scaly tail. Leon was lifted from the ground and thrown toward the far wall like a rag doll. The soldiers approached the creature. It stood, thumping its tail on the floor.

No one dared move. It cast a lizard-like glance at Mya. "Let's go," it said and bent down, gnashing its teeth and reaching for Mya.

She felt a movement from behind her. Zach, as quick as a cat, grabbed the creature's head and pulled it down further with one hand. Taken off guard, the creature fell forward. Zach swung the dagger with the other hand and pierced the creature's skull.

It roared once more and collapsed to the floor, black liquid leaking out of the wound on its head. In a short moment, its body dissolved into a large wormy puddle.

As soon as the creature died, the spell on Mya broke. Zach darted over and grabbed her just before her knees buckled.

CHAPTER 22

She cupped his face with her hands. "You didn't die. Why?" She smiled at him.

"Did you want me to?" He smiled back.

"But I saw—"

He pressed a kiss on her lips to stop her from talking.

Someone had let Dan out of the cell. He walked toward Zach, cursing. Zach turned and looked at him. "You should thank me for locking you in. Now you don't have to explain to anyone that the reason you don't get involved in fights is because you don't approve violence—and not because you're a chicken."

"And you think throwing yourself at drawn weapons is sensible?" Dan said.

Zach shrugged. "It worked."

Mya looked at the gash on Zach's arm. From the wound, red blood seeped out instead of the silver substance. "It's only a seal. Ayana moved it when she gave me the wristband. Because it's such a critical point in my body, I'm trying not to advertise its new location." He grinned at Mya. When she didn't return the smile, he frowned. "What's up?"

"Why did you do that?' she asked him.

"I knew someone from the multiverse wanted you, so I came up with a little plot to figure out who had an interest in capturing you."

She smiled. "Thank you. But it's not relevant now."

"Why not?"

"I'm a deity, Zach." She looked into his eyes, gauging his reaction.

He smiled. "I told you I'm half alien. Now you're telling me you're a deity. If we're in competition for weirdness, you win. But why isn't my attempt to lure out the person who wants you from the multiverse relevant?"

"To get people here to save you, I promised Ishtar I would come back and serve as a deity under her forever." She felt a lump in her throat now.

"Ishtar, the Goddess of love and war?" Dan asked.

Mya nodded.

"Nasty!" Dan muttered.

"What?" Mya exclaimed.

Dan said nothing further, but he looked at Zach and shook his head slightly. Zach's eyes grew intense. She knew he was going to do something he'd regret.

Leon approached and poured out a stream of Babylonian. He said if Mya didn't make it back to the court this time, Ishtar would kill her. Nobody stood this Goddess up, and Mya had already done that once.

But Zach didn't speak Babylonian, and Leon didn't speak English. So the conversation, or lack thereof, didn't go anywhere.

Zach held her shoulder. "Mya, I can only think of two reasons you should go with me. One, you know my feelings for you. Two, your Goddess isn't going to protect you. She's playing a power game in which you're a pawn. Someone or something from the multiverse wants you, and your Goddess is going to trade you for her benefit."

"How do you know that?" A tear rolled down her face.

"You know a lot about this, Dan. Please tell her."

Dan nodded. "In a nutshell, legend suggests that your Goddess always played double-crossing games. She would do it to her friends, family, and lovers. You're her deity. You can't be worth that much to her. I'm sorry."

"But that's all speculation, isn't it?"

Zach raked his hands through his hair. "Whatever it is you're doing for your Goddess, is it because you owe her something?"

Mya nodded.

"You must have come close to paying if off at some point. Didn't you notice you never seemed to be able to pay it off?" Zach asked.

"I don't know."

"You should know. It's a classic power game. She will never let you pay it off. You'll owe her for the rest of eternity. Come with me. I'll negotiate a way out for you. If I can't, our king will be able to do it. Eudaiz is a very significant universe. Your Goddess should have some respect for us."

She looked at him. She had never seen green eyes so striking, so compelling. She believed every word he said. She believed he would make her happy. He would protect her. She had never had this kind of offer of protection in her life.

Another tear rolled down her face.

Zach pressed a button on his wrist unit. A portal opened right outside the window of the building. They could just walk right into it. Under the bright light of the portal, he looked like a dark angel. He reached his hand out for her. "Come with me, Mya."

She smiled and reached her hand out to his.

When their fingertips were close to one another, Leon exclaimed, "Ishtar will seek revenge. This will damage her ego, and she will never let this go. You're creating a war between the two universes, Mylittle."

She stopped and withdrew her hand.

She could see Zach didn't understand a word Leon just said, but he could tell the impact the speech had on her. He curled his fingers back and withdrew his hand. Then, as fast as lightning, he pulled his knife, swiveled, grabbed Leon, and pressed the knife to his throat. "Mya, step inside the teleport with Dan, or I'll shove this knife into his throat. This isn't your doing—it's on me."

"Don't do this, Zach."

"If you go back to court, you'll be handed over to whoever was dealing with your Goddess. I'm not going to let that happen. Step inside the teleport, Mya."

Mya stepped inside the teleport and stood next to Dan. Zach shoved Leon away. Then he closed the teleport. In a short moment, all Mya saw was a bright light.

***

Outside the teleport was a magnificent rolling hillside. Mya had never felt such genuine peace in her life, even during good times. Now she wondered whether Zach's speculation was right. Ishtar was the Goddess of love and war, but during the entire time she had served the Goddess, she had only seen war—both on a galactic scale and a personal scale.

The Goddess was in constant war—even with herself.

Zach looked at her. His eyes were pensive, striking, and more focused than ever. "Shouldn't you slap me in the face for forcing you to come here?"

"That's what ordinary girls do. I'm not ordinary." She smiled.

"That's right. You're a deity. A good one. You'd rather jeopardize your chances for freedom than risk innocent lives."

"Are we in Eudaiz? You said it's at war. This is so peaceful."

"No, this is the Daimon Gate."

"Oh, the neutral gateway between universes. I know of it and have arranged for a number of my subjects to get here. I've never been myself."

Zach grinned. "Then I don't have to explain anything. You know you'll be safe here. Even your Goddess has no access to this place. I have arranged a guest pass. You are a guest of the Daimon Gate. No one in the multiverse will be able to touch you here."

"When did you arrange this?"

He smiled and said nothing.

"Before you came back? How confident you were that I was coming here with you!"

He merely smiled. But the smile quickly faded. "I have to go back to Eudaiz. Will you wait for me here?"

More than a thousand years ago, on her first mission, she had arranged a peace treaty that had resulted in the massacre of thousands of innocents. Nadinn, the tribe leader, had said the blood debt was on her and that it would come back for her.

For more than a thousand years, she had never been able to work off that debt. And even if she had, she would never be able to forget that bloody afternoon. There had been the smell of wildflowers and wet grass—the smell of a good and prosperous season. And then the air that carried the aura of a dead battlefield had haunted her for those thousand years.

What had those women said to their loved ones before the men went to sign the treaty and never came back? Was that what she was doing with Zach right now?

She had believed in the difference between good and evil. Between right and wrong. And she still did. She had done everything she could do for the tribal war. If she had to do it again, the peace treaty would always be her solution. But when humans betrayed one another, there was nothing she could do to help.

She knew she was no ordinary woman. She knew Zach was not just a soldier. He was smart. He was built to lead. He had promised to come back to her. That was the only thing she'd need.

She would wait.

She smiled and nodded. "I will."

Zach pulled her into his arms. They kissed each other like they kissed for the first time. She would make sure that every kiss would be like the first time, because she would never know when his name would be up on any list.

PART TWO

CHAPTER 23

The shiny floor of the Babylonian Court reflected her shadow. Mya could clearly see the modern outfit she wore—her skinny jeans, her pointy heels, the soft silky blouse that flattered her figure, and her one-of-a-kind leather jacket.

The first time she had forgotten to change into her ridiculous golden bikini-like outfit to attend court, she panicked. But not this time. And it wasn't because she had done this before. It was because she had come here to die.

It was never a good day to die. But she deserved to do it in her favorite outfits when her time was up.

As much as she had sworn to herself she wouldn't think of Zach, she still did. This wasn't his fault. It wasn't her fault, either.

She'd waited for him in the Daimon Gate as she had promised. He hadn't come back, but that didn't mean he wouldn't.

Then the message from Ishtar came.

After so many years working for Ishtar, she should have known. Zach was right that her Goddess couldn't touch her if she stayed in the Daimon Gate—the most powerful neutral universe in the cosmos. But that didn't stop Ishtar from sending her an ultimatum.

If she didn't go back to court, Ishtar would reverse all of Mya's cases from the last thousand years. That meant the evils she had killed would return, and the innocents she had saved would die.

She couldn't message Zach. Eudaiz was at war, and because of that, the communication device Zach had given her was unresponsive.

Mya cursed silently. Her Goddess knew her too well. Left with no choice, Mya had come back to court to face certain death.

***

In the middle of the fighting ground, Leon grinned in satisfaction. He had won. After such a long time as the temple guard, he'd thought his combat skills were gone. But he proved himself to be a competent warrior after all. He looked at the blood pooling on the sandy ground of the Well of the Death and kicked at the monstrous two-headed lizard one more time to assure himself it was really dead.

Ishtar had sentenced him to death after he had broken the news that Mya wouldn't come back. He hadn't revealed her location, but he was sure Ishtar would find out somehow.

He thought he was only a messenger and should be fine. But Ishtar—the Goddess of love and war—had shown no mercy. Mya, who had seen only the warlike side of Ishtar, had been right the whole time. But that was irrelevant. He would have been dead if he hadn't won this fight. But he had. He killed the monster at the bottom of the well.

Leon shook his head, thinking about how much Ishtar loved games.

His adrenaline surged in waves through his mind and body. He was still drunk from the sensation of his unexpected victory. The gate opened for him, but as he approached it, a daunting feeling weighed heavily on his chest. Something was wrong.

At the gate, instead of giving clearance for him to exit, a group of soldiers marched toward him, splitting into two rows as they approached. In between the rows stood Ishtar, adorned in her war regalia, looking at him with a half-smile on her face.

She was challenging him.

It was totally ludicrous. Even if she fought him using only one pinky finger, he was not supposed to defeat her. *How is this a fair game?* he wondered.

He looked up at the stretch of limestone at the top of the well which reflected the sunlight. Leon had always loved the court. He had always been proud of what he did. Until now.

"My Goddess!" He bowed.

"How many times have you been a witness to this fight to the death? You know there are *two* rounds," said Ishtar.

"I had forgotten, Ishtar."

She smiled. "Don't worry. I will remind you."

He opened his mouth, about to say something. But before a single word came out, a curved dagger flew in his direction. If he hadn't ducked quickly, his throat would have been sliced open. Although it missed his throat, the sharp blade of the knife cut into his arm. Blood spurted out.

"Ishtar!" he whispered in shock.

"Why are you so surprised?"

"I don't deserve this...I didn't do anything wrong."

The Goddess shook her head. "You favor Mya. That's what you did wrong."

"I never knew feeling fondness for a person was wrong, Ishtar."

"It's when you act on that fondness and let Mya go free to a place where you know I can't reach her that it becomes unacceptable."

"It wasn't my doing, Ishtar!" That was all he got out before his body spun in the air and smashed down onto the harsh, hot sand of the well bottom. The Goddess approached and thrust the knife at him. He grabbed the sharp blade with his bare hands and watched his blood flow down between his fingers.

He knew he was going to die, but he would try to do one last good thing before he finished. "If you kill me, will you forgive Mya?"

"It's not for you to decide." Ishtar grunted out the words and pressed the knife harder against his throat.

"There isn't a second round in this challenge, Ishtar. I won. If you kill me, do you think this incident won't be reported to your Gods?"

"You're threatening me?" She gave him a hard kick. After all these years you served my court, you should know by now that I conform to no one, and I make the rules. Those who follow my rules will live. I have reserved a very special place in hell for the others."

She charged several blows on him using her Goddess's power. He felt as if his body was going to disintegrate.

"I have been a loyal servant to you for a very long time. Doesn't that count for anything?"

He swore he saw tears in Ishtar's eyes. That was unprecedented. She pressed the knife to his throat with more force. "Someone has to pay for what Mya did. You are fond of her, so let that person be you."

Leon closed his eyes and waited for the knife to puncture his jugular.

The sound of the gate opening stopped the blade. He heard a voice announcing Mya had come back to court and was awaiting Ishtar.

As the knife was withdrawn from his throat, Leon opened his eyes and thought he saw relief wash across Ishtar's eyes.

"Today is your lucky day," she muttered then turned on her heel and left through the gate. Leon remained on the sand a while longer, digesting what had just happened.

When he looked up to the top of the well, he saw a shadow flit across the limestone. It withdrew quickly before he could get a better look.

CHAPTER 24

Zach didn't like what he saw. The chill air cut into his skin. It was painful—not because of the ice pieces in the wind, nor because of the eerie aura, but because of the emptiness in it. He knew Mya wasn't there before he even searched for her. He was late, and it pained him to know she had gone before he got back.

"Where are you, Mya?" he asked the wind.

She had promised to wait for him in the Daimon Gate. Why didn't she? He hadn't known her for long. Hell, apart from knowing she was a woman with many secrets, he didn't know her at all. He hadn't expected her to wait here for him for the rest of her life. But he thought they had built something together that deserved a little bit of patience on her side.

Zach paced back and forth, searching the small cottage on the hillside where he had arranged for her to stay. There was no sign of Mya. The furniture stared at him in silence. The kitchen was so neat he wondered if she'd used it at all.

There was a small table in the middle of the room. On top of it, a tea set was neatly arranged. He walked around the table, observing the tea set. Then he glanced quickly at the corner of the room. Stepping back to gain some momentum, he flew at the cabinet in the corner, swinging a hard kick to its door.

The cabinet crumbled, and a creature jumped out—a human-sized frog that stood upright on two legs.

Zach grabbed it before it fled and threw its slimy body down on the table. He pulled his dagger and stabbed through the web between its fingers, pinning one hand to the table. It cried out in pain and poured out a stream of strange language. Zach rolled his eyes and switched on his wrist unit's translator function. A computer voice spoke, "Please don't kill me! I'm just a messenger."

"Where are you from?" Zach asked, and the computer again translated.

"Xiilok," the creature said.

"What message did you bring Mya?"

"I can't tell you."

Zach slammed its head on the table.

"I can't tell you. Please don't kill me!" it cried again.

"Maybe some tea will open your throat," Zach grunted and grabbed the teapot.

The creature bit its lips closed to seal its mouth. Yellow liquid streamed from its eyes—the equivalent of human tears, Zach surmised.

"Mya doesn't drink tea, you stupid Xiilok creature. You hoped I would take a sip while I waited for her, didn't you? What sort of poison did you put in it?"

"No, no. Not poison. Just a sleeping potion to buy me some time to get away."

Zach pulled his dagger up and stabbed down again.

The creature squealed.

"You think I'm stupid? You had no idea when I would get here. If you wanted to leave, you could have left. But you didn't—you waited around for me, and you set up this stupid tea set. I don't believe you're just a messenger."

Zach pulled out another dagger.

"Oh, no, no. I am! I'm really only a messenger!"

"Right. So what was the message then?" He pressed his dagger to the creature's temple. "And please don't make me repeat my question."

"Someone paid me to tell Mya that Zach Flynn had been captured in Xiilok. They wanted me to tell her they're willing to trade him for some information... That's all I know. I don't even know who paid me. The job was on the market, and I grabbed it. The client was anonymous. Please don't kill me..." More yellow liquid ran from the creature's eyes.

"And did you deliver the message to her?" Zach removed his hand from the creature's head and wiped the yellow liquid that had smeared on his knuckles on his pants in disgust.

The creature shook his head. "When I got here, she had already gone. But I had taken the payment—and I don't want to give it back—so I waited around. I hoped to catch some of her associates to make up for the loss."

Where did she go? Zach contemplated. This creature obviously didn't know who he was, so it had to be at the lower end of the chain of command. Mya was a deity and would be protected by the goddess she was working for. Someone or something wanted her to be excluded from that protection so they could grab her, possibly at the transitional zone of the multiverse.

For a moment, Zach forgot the creature in front of him.

Then he saw a flash of movement from the corner of his eyes. The green creature leaped at him. He swiveled around and swung his dagger, slashing at its abdomen. It hissed and withdrew. Its skin toughened and darkened and grew scales. A row of pointy teeth popped out of its gaping mouth. The creature's head transformed into a lizard-like head. It hissed louder.

Zach didn't hesitate. He shoved the dagger into its chest, pinning it to the wall before it could make another move at him.

The creature convulsed. He knew it would soon die, turning into a worm-filled puddle. "You'd look better dead as a frog," Zach muttered and pulled his dagger out. As he predicted, the creature slumped to the floor, lifeless.

He hadn't been to Xiilok, but he knew it was the land of the multiversal outlaws.

Then he noticed the puddle on the ground. Unlike other Xiilok creatures that would have disintegrated into a wormy puddle by now, this dead lizard had left only a pile of ugly, scaly skin on the ground.

He crouched and used the leg of a chair to lift up the skin. On the ground beneath it was something that looked like an electronic device the size of a tennis ball.

"What the hell?" Zach muttered. "A Xiilok robot?" He shook his head. He had always thought of Xiilok as a purely magical land, but apparently they had technology as well!

"Let's see what you've got here." He switched the scanning function of his wrist unit on. A beam of blue laser scanned the ball. He could see the stream of data it imported. When the strings of text appeared on the screen of his wrist unit, he read what they said. And his blood ran cold.

CHAPTER 25

Mya stared at the small jar sitting on a golden tray in front of her. She looked up at Ishtar, who leaned back nonchalantly on her throne as if what was happening in her court at the moment meant nothing.

The poison in the jar reeked. But that wasn't what made Mya wince. It was the aloofness of Ishtar that hurt the most. All those years she had served in the court meant nothing. She shifted her gaze from the jar to Ishtar and waited. Nothing. No reaction.

Mya nodded and picked up the jar.

Ishtar cleared her throat. "Is there anything you want to say to anyone?"

"I've spent more of my life outside the court than inside. There is no one here with whom I would want to leave a message. But may I ask for one final favor, my goddess?"

Ishtar shifted on her throne. Then she waved her hand absently. "Granted."

"I'd like to ask for a pardon for Leon. I know he will be punished for coming back to court without me."

Ishtar looked at her for a long moment then nodded. "All right. I grant a pardon to Leon. I'll let him live."

Mya nodded. She looked at the jar she was holding and raised it. Her motion was halted by the sound of chaos echoing in. She put the poison back down and turned around. Leon had shoved the guards away and marched into the court.

The guards didn't really respond in turn. Mya knew they respected Leon as head of the temple guards. He walked straight into the court to stand next to Mya.

"I hold you in contempt of court, Leon!" Ishtar raised her voice.

"If I let Mya die, I'm a dead man walking. I no longer fear the court's formality, my goddess."

Ishtar slammed her palm down on the arm of her chair. "How dare you!"

"Leon, you don't have to do this," Mya said.

He looked at her. "All creatures have to die someday. You came back to spare the lives of the strangers you saved over a thousand years. If I can trade my life to spare yours, I will. I guarded this temple for a long time. Apparently my work didn't count for much." He glanced at Ishtar as he said, "If you were out there, Mya, you could save a lot more lives."

"Guards!" Ishtar shouted.

There was no response.

"Guards, take these two out and throw them into the well," Ishtar ordered.

Not a single guard moved.

Ishtar stood up. "You are forming a coup in my court, Leon? Do you know the consequences of making me angry?"

"I dare not, my Goddess. If you let Mya live, I am yours. You can do whatever you want with me."

Ishtar laughed insanely and waved her arm. The guards standing at the entrance to the temple clutched at their throats, slumped to the floor, burst into flames, and died.

Mya dropped to her knees. "Please don't kill them, my Goddess. Please forgive them."

"She won't, Mya," Leon said and copped a lightning strike from Ishtar. His body was thrown to the far end of the room, and he rolled across the shiny floor.

"Please don't kill him, Ishtar!" Mya crawled toward the tray with the poison. "If this is what you want—"

From the entrance of the temple, the guard announced, "Zach Flynn has requested to enter the court." The guard rushed in and handed Ishtar a tablet.

"What is this?" Ishtar asked, frowning and reading the text on the tablet at the same time.

"That's the equivalent of an invitation scroll in your world," Zach said in English and entered the court. His wrist unit translated his words into Babylonian.

Mya looked up at him. He was formidable, like a magnificent warrior walking into the court with authority. He looked at her and nodded slightly, but he didn't make a move. Something in him had changed. He would normally have rushed over to help her up from the floor. B\ut at that moment, he locked his eyes with Ishtar's. She stood still, her face reddening.

Mya scrambled up from the floor and rushed toward Leon to make sure he was all right. She helped him stand up and walk toward the center of the court. Zach was still in a staring contest with Ishtar. Mya knew he was using his sound waves, but she said nothing.

Soon, the water jar on a small table next to Ishtar exploded.

"Impressive," Ishtar muttered.

Zach smiled.

Ishtar put the tablet on the table. "Just a short while ago, you were a subject that one of my minor deities had to save. Now you come here as Sciphil Two of Eudaiz. Should I check that fact?"

"You could, Ishtar. But it would take time for you to do so as I don't believe the technology you use here is quite up to the standards of the multiversal system. If anything happens to Mya, the relationship between Eudaiz and your court will be tarnished. I trust you wouldn't like that."

Ishtar narrowed her eyes. "How so? I know Eudaiz is powerful. But I don't see any benefits in our association."

"I'm not talking about benefits. I'm talking about the damage a poor relationship between our two universes could cause."

"I see." Ishtar leaned back. "Do elaborate."

"Someone in Xiilok has an interest in obtaining a potion you lost more than a thousand years ago, Earth time." Zach smiled.

Ishtar shifted in her chair.

"Apparently, Mya was responsible for the loss of that potion," said Zach. "That's why she has worked for more than a thousand years to pay off her debts. Which she never will because you won't let her."

"She let him go. That's why she's responsible." Ishtar spoke between clenched teeth. Everyone could feel the floor of the temple shaking. She was getting angry.

Mya approached. "Stop talking, Zach. She'll kill you whether it's right or wrong."

A column at the far end of the temple exploded and crumbled into dust.

Zach ignored Ishtar's budding temper and raised his voice above the noise. "By *him*, do you mean Nunnaki, your lover?"

A lightning bolt struck in Zach's direction. He swiveled and at the same time narrowed his eyes at Ishtar's chair. The lightning missed Zach and dug a large crater in the ground. At the same time, Ishtar's throne crumbled, sending her tumbling to the floor. She stood up, even angrier.

Mya jumped in front of Zach. "Ishtar, please calm down. If this is all about that missing jar, I'll go and find the potion for you."

"It's not just a missing jar!" Ishtar screamed.

Zach pulled Mya behind him. "You may have been isolated in your court for a long time, Goddess. You are powerful. But your power cannot raise you above your superiors. You chose not to tell them the truth. But once you have committed an action, it is documented in the multiverse, and your superiors know about it."

"Documented by whom?" Ishtar roared.

"By technology, Ishtar. Have you heard of the EYE, the most sophisticated and independent computer system in the multiverse?"

"It belongs to the Daimon Gate, and no one— including your king—has access."

Zach smiled. "So you do know of it. Well, you're right. I don't have access." He turned and winked at Mya. "But I do know this. You secretly made a potion that could raise the dead, and you did it against your superior's permission. Your lover, Nunnaki, stole your potion and ran. You asked Mya to give chase, and Mya let him go on grounds of compassion and because she thought it was just a jar of medicine, not a forbidden potion."

Ishtar stepped down from the platform of her throne.

Mya darted forward. "My goddess, I'll find the potion for you. Zach's a councillor of Eudaiz. When I was in the Daimon Gate, I Eudaiz's power. You don't want to go against them."

Ishtar narrowed her eyes. "Why would Eudaiz care about my little jar of potion?"

Zach shook his head. "We don't. But our king has just been crowned, and during the coronation process, he destroyed one of the most notorious evils in the multiverse. And that evil needs your potion to revive his power."

"So your king doesn't want the potion to get into his enemy's hands. If I send Mya to go after it, does that mean I'm doing your king a favor?"

Zach laughed. "The current king of Eudaiz is Ciaran LeBlanc. You can look up the records when you get a chance. But for now, let me say this—he doesn't need your favor. He'd already discussed it with your superiors. The potion not only needs to be retrieved, but it needs to be protected. And Eudaiz is the safest place. Also, before Nunnaki died—"

"He died?"

For the first time in her life, Mya saw tears in Ishtar's eyes.

Zach nodded. "The evil I mentioned is Hoyt Flanagan. He's a sorcerer. He knows what he needs, and he knows what to do with the potion. He captured Nunnaki. To protect the secret of the potion's whereabouts, Nunnaki killed himself. But before he died, he made Mya the potion's guardian. Only she can call it up if she finds it."

"He killed himself?" A tear rolled down Ishtar's face. She turned away for a long moment before turning back.

"If you find the potion and bring it back here, I'm willing to forgive all of your debts, Mya."

"I'd like to help," Leon said.

"Great—the more, the merrier," Zach muttered.

"I'll bring the potion back to court, my goddess," Mya said. Then she bowed and withdrew. Leon did the same. Zach turned on his heel and strode out behind them. Ishtar left the court without saying another word.

CHAPTER 26

Wagga Wagga burned with the heat of a dry summer wind as they walked along the street toward a hotel. It was a small and charming town close to the Australian outback territory. Mya had been based in Australia for at least five decades, but she had never claimed to know the country, especially the outback. She was too busy to travel, and her work had kept her mostly around central downtown.

The least conspicuous way of entering town was for Zach to teleport them there during the night. They'd enter on the outskirts of town and travel on foot just as dawn broke through the sky. Zach took Mya and Leon to a guest house in the middle of town. He said nothing during their travels, and her mind was flooded with millions of questions.

Zach took Mya to her room. "I'll hire a car, and we'll go to the site tonight," he said and turned to leave.

"Hey!" she called out and waved her arms in the air.

"Yes?"

"Don't you think I need some kind of explanation? How do you know all this? Where are we going?"

He turned and looked at her. Then he closed the door and sat down on a small chair next to the coffee table. It was a quite cozy hotel room, and Zach's size took up a significant part of it. He ruffled his hands through his hair. Not a good sign. Mya narrowed her eyes at him.

He looked at her with his soft green eyes. "I bluffed most of it."

She blew out her held breath. She needed to sit, so she plopped down on a corner of the bed. She inhaled and exhaled and then said, "I need to know which part you didn't bluff..." She inhaled again. "To see if we can leverage."

He nodded. "I came back to the cottage in the Daimon Gate and couldn't find you. I found a Xiilok creature there instead. When I killed it, I found a chip inside its body that contained data about Nunnaki, the Goddess, and the possible location of the potion."

She waited. When she received silence rather than further information, she asked, "Is that all?"

He shrugged. "The creature reported that he had missed your arrival at the cottage, and you seemed to have gone back to the court. When I listened to the data chip from the creature, your name was mentioned as the only reason Nunnaki was able to escape the court. So I dug a bit further into the data, put two and two together and made up the rest."

"That's a hell of a lot more than two and two." She stood but couldn't pace back and forth because the room was too small. "What if your bluff didn't work? Do you know Ishtar could kill you? What took you so long anyway? I thought you weren't coming back..."

He stepped over to her, held her shoulders, and looked into her eyes. "I promised you I'd come back for you."

She pushed him against the wall and ravished his mouth. His breath quickened. Her heart raced. His hands searched her body, sneaked inside her blouse in search of her warm flesh. She tugged at his shirt.

But then he suddenly stopped. He grabbed her hands before she could peel off his shirt.

"What? I've seen your body before. Did you lose your six-pack?" she joked.

He chuckled. "No, it's just not the right time..."

She threw him to the bed and yanked his shirt off as he went down. She hopped on the bed, flipped him over, and straddled him before he knew what was happening. And then she saw it. An eight-inch scar on his chest, the unmistakable remnant of a stab wound right at the position of his heart.

She stopped and stared. Then tears rolled down her face. She climbed off him. He sat up and pulled her into his arms.

"It's okay," he said. "I told you Eudaiz was at war before I left."

"You couldn't have survived that injury." She looked into his eyes.

He shook his head. "I didn't." He wiped the tears off her face. "That's why Ishtar could see on the record I came as Sciphil Two. I was only a successor before, remember?"

She nodded.

"I was supposed to die from this wound. But Ayana wouldn't accept it. She was injured, too. The

Sciphil chamber can heal only one of us, and that one person has to be a proper Sciphil. She transferred the role to me. And she died because of that."

She embraced him and felt every ounce of muscle in his body vibrate with emotion. "I'm sorry. That must have been difficult for you."

They held each other for a while. Then he nodded. "I can't imagine being a deity is easy, either. Let's just say we're equal now." He smiled. "I'm a Eudaizian. And being a Sciphil means I'm responsible for several million citizens in my district. I no longer have the liberty to travel back and forth between Earth and Eudaiz. So after we finish this, I'd like you to come back with me to Eudaiz."

"What will I do there?"

He smiled. "I'll find you a job." He pushed her down to the bed and bent over her to kiss her.

There was a sudden loud banging noise from next door, and Leon's voice echoed in from his room. He was shouting at someone, and the words were incoherent. They scrambled to their feet and stormed out of Mya's room in the direction of the commotion.

CHAPTER 27

Mya and Zach charged into Leon's room, finding him lying on the floor. A naked man with a knife in his hand stood next to Leon. Mya's heart went numb. Before Zach charged at him, the man turned around, shifted into a gigantic cat, and leaped out the window. Mya rushed toward Leon. Zach was about to give chase after the cat but decided against it. He stepped outside the room to talk to the staff, who had arrived because they'd heard the noise.

Mya checked Leon. He was breathing, and it appeared he had no fatal wound.

"Leon," she called and shook his shoulders. His eyes fluttered and opened.

"Mya!" he said from the ground.

"How are you feeling?" She smiled and helped him up.

Leon glanced around, dazed. "Where's the cat?"

"You let a shapeshifter into your room thinking it was a cat?"

"It looked just like one of those big cats I trained at the court. I know them well."

Mya realized that not only did Leon not speak the language, he had also never mixed in with the current human civilization. He had always served the Babylonian court. She didn't know exactly how the court and the human world interacted, but she knew that regardless of how much the court had developed, the Babylonian civilization had departed from the human world a long time ago, and the two had never crossed paths again.

"Leon, the cats you trained at court were real animals. What you saw just then was a shapeshifter, and it knocked you out."

Leon grimaced. "I don't remember that happening. Cats are gentle. They don't act like that."

Mya shook her head. "Okay, Leon. But listen, Zach knows where we can find the potion. We'll go there tonight. After we get it, I'm taking you back to the court."

"What's the hurry?"

"You can't mix with Earth creatures. Humans or animals."

"Why not?"

"Stop asking questions. Just do what I say. It's best for you."

He nodded. "All right."

Mya helped him stand up. Leon took a quick self-inventory and found himself to be fine.

"What's a shapeshifter?" he asked.

"It's a magical creature that can change into different shapes." The computer translated Zach's response into Babylonian. Mya turned around.

"You're a believer, Zach?" She smiled.

"I don't have a choice. It's not a matter of believing. It's a matter of explaining what's happening in the multiverse. Having been to many universes, nothing surprises me anymore."

They heard several low growls vibrating in the air.

"It's too confined in here. Get out," Zach said and pulled Mya outside. Leon followed. When they got out to the narrow corridor, two leopards approached from the left and three from the right. Their eyes sparkled with a bizarre green shade.

"You said they aren't normal cats, Mya?" Leon asked.

"They aren't," Mya said.

Two janitors rushed into the corridor. One of them pointed. "There, I told you I saw those wild cats." They pulled their guns.

"Don't worry, we'll handle this," the other janitor said to Zach, Mya, and Leon. Two of the leopards turned around and leaped at the janitors. They fired their guns, but the bullets didn't stop the cats. In no time, the janitors became piles of torn flesh. The other three leopards rushed at Zach, Mya, and Leon.

"They're mine!" Leon yelled in anger. He pushed Zach and Mya back, pulled two knives out of his boot, and ran at the leopards. Leon was agile, and the narrow corridor didn't do the animals any good. With the combat skills Leon had acquired from several years of combat training, he easily overcame the leopards, turning them into nothing more than piles of meat.

Three of the animals shifted back into naked men before they died.

"He's good!" Zach muttered.

"Ishtar does have a knack for picking talent," said Mya.

"Yeah, that's why she chose you." Zach winked at her.

They heard the crackling noise of burning electrical wires. Fire sparked out from the control room at the end of the corridor.

"Run!" Zach shouted and tugged at Mya. They ran down the corridor and outside the building just as it exploded in a gigantic ball of fire.

"This is going to cause a bushfire. Mya, can you use your deity magic to put out the fire?" Zach asked.

"Sure," she said, turning and running away from him.

"Where are you going?" Zach yelled. She ran so fast he couldn't catch her.

"She runs like the wind," Leon said. "And she can't make it rain if that's what you're wondering."

Mya charged into a lonely phone booth standing at the side of the country road and slammed her hand on the emergency button.

"We need a fire brigade!" she shouted into the phone.

CHAPTER 28

Kirra gazed out at the red dirt road leading to her cabin. She wasn't the boss in this hiking camp that organized tours to the outback of Australia for adventurous and savvy travelers, but she had enough authority that she only had to take the tours she wanted. She was a good tour guide, and in this economy, they took any tour they could get. They needed her.

But Zach Flynn was no ordinary tourist.

A single encounter with him a decade ago had scarred her for life. He had left an empty place in her—one she hadn't been able to fill for many years. She traveled a bit, always keeping an eye out for him. And she'd had relationships on and off. But she had never been able to find the fire Zach had in any other man. The passionate fire he had for music, art, love, and life, and his genuine devotion to beauty. For a while, she had been able to accept the fact that she wouldn't be able to find that in any other man. She had adjusted to that realization and had become happy with what she had, returning to this stretch of the woods and her old job.

And now, here he was again.

But why?

The campsite they had assigned him in his last trip had burned to the ground. The host and his family had died in the fire. Zach had been traumatized witnessing the event and had left without saying a word to her. So why was he coming back?

She shook her head.

When she received the list of expected guests, she couldn't believe her eyes. She had looked for him everywhere over the years without success. And here he was, falling right into her lap.

From the window of the cabin she used as her office, she saw an SUV roll into the driveway. It was covered in so much red dirt that she couldn't tell the color of the vehicle. From the driver's side, Zach stepped out.

Kirra withheld a gasp. Time had agreed well with him. It had been several years, but her hormones still surged to an alarming level just by looking at him. He walked over and opened the passenger door. And out stepped a woman who shattered all of her hopes of ever being in competition for Zach.

Well, it's not like she was in any kind of competition. He didn't even know she had a thing for him. She had been eighteen back then. To him, she'd been only a sweet little girl. But now, she was mature enough to— Her daydream halted at the sight of an angel exiting the car from the backseat.

Absently, she cleared her throat. Maybe he wasn't an angel because there was still daylight, and she was one hundred percent awake. But he was the perfect example of one straight from the pages of the Bible—tall, lean, golden hair, milky skin, and a perfectly sculptured face with gentle blue eyes.

Kirra frowned. She had never read the Bible, so where had that image come from? But after a short moment contemplating, she remembered. She had read books in the library with pictures of angels. There had actually been a time in her past when she'd had to plant her backside down in a library to study ancient civilizations associated with popular tourist attractions. She'd hated every moment she had to spend there, but apparently, to get a license and clients with repeat business, she had to at least know the places for which she was going to serve as a guide.

Before she realized it, the angelic man was leaning against the wall right outside her cabin door. When Zach and the woman went into the reception area to finalize their bookings, the man braced his hands against the wall of her cabin and then pounded one hand a couple of times against it.

She opened the door. He was startled and withdrew. His face started to redden.

"Hi, I'm Kirra. I think I'm your tour guide." She reached her hand out for a handshake.

He paused for second, stared at her, then fumbled with his pocket and pulled out a small book—the title said *English for Travelers*. He flipped through the pages then looked at her and said, "Hi, how you do?" in a very strong and strange accent. He shook his head and said again, "Hi, how do you do? I am Leon."

She grinned.

Catching the signal that he must have said it right, he smiled and reached his hand out for a handshake.

What a smile! she thought.

"Here you are!" said a sultry and exotic female voice from behind Leon. He was tall and had blocked her view, so she hadn't seen Zach and the woman coming.

"You've made a lady friend already, Leon!" She turned toward Zach. "See, I told you Leon could use that book. He's a fast learner."

Zach chuckled. "I'm sure the clothes you bought him have nothing do with him hitting on the first lady he met in the outback." Zach smiled at Kirra.

"Come on, give him some credit. He's very fast," Mya said and then turned toward Kirra. "Hi, I'm Mya. And this is Zach. You must be Kirra. The reception desk told us you're our tour guide."

Kirra blinked and looked at Zach. He approached, and his eyes paused on her face for a long moment. *He doesn't remember me...great!* she thought.

Then Zach grinned. It was the same unmistakable brilliant smile of his. "Kirra Jane Poleski, how wonderful you look!" He bent down and hugged her.

Not only had he remembered her, he'd also remembered her *middle* name.

"How are you, Zach? It's been such a long time," she said.

"Indeed. It's a pity we're not even staying the night," Zach said.

"You're not going to the cave now, are you?" She raised an eyebrow.

Zach frowned. "That's exactly what we're going to do. We just rented some camping gear from you guys, and we're leaving before dark."

"No, you can't. There's a dust storm coming, and the cave will be right in the eye of it. I know you're experienced, Zach. But dust storms are dangerous. You don't want to put your friends in the middle of it."

Zach looked at Mya and Leon then back at Kirra. She shared with him the weather report and warning she had just received.

"Stay the night. It's on me." Kirra smiled.

Zach looked at Mya. She nodded. He looked disappointed but then nodded as well. "I'll check in at the reception desk," he said and headed in that direction. Mya followed him.

From the corner of her eyes, Kirra saw a shadow in the woods and then a pair of glimmering green eyes. If she wasn't mistaken, they were the eyes of a wild cat. They had never come this close to the campsite before. Regardless of what people said about how dangerous they were, she thought they were actually quite shy.

She frowned at the shadow.

Leon turned in the direction she was looking. As soon as he caught sight of the eyes, he ran in that direction.

"Hey!" she called, but he didn't listen to her. She ran back into her cabin and grabbed her hunting rifle and a tranquilizer dart. Then she raced after Leon.

CHAPTER 29

Elanora tapped her long, manicured fingernails on the edge of the stone table. She didn't shift much these days, so she could afford to decorate her nails and wear outfits that didn't facilitate shape-shifting. She was the upcoming alpha of the wild cat clan. And regardless of all the myths about how they were required to shift and run often or risk losing their wild instincts, her kind didn't need to.

She liked her human appearance—wild, long black hair, striking dark eyes, and tall with curves that could stir the loin of any human male she came across. She chuckled, thinking about humans and the myths they believed in. When there wasn't much information available, people tended to rely on whatever information they had, she supposed— legend, folklore, fairy tales, and rumor.

Her clan wasn't comprised of ordinary cats. They weren't cats like those in the fairyland, nor were they typical were-creatures. But she knew what humans labeled them—were-leopards. As if there were such creatures.

She pulled out a stack of paper one of her minions had given her. Hundreds of images of artifacts, jars of potion, jewelry, and treasure maps. She smiled to herself. She hadn't received good news like this in a very long time. The people of the forgotten Babylonian court had fallen right into her lap.

She reached out for her phone and punched in a number. At the other end of the line, the receptionist of the travel lodge answered with a chirpy greeting.

"It's me," Elanora said.

"Yes, Elanora," the receptionist answered shakily. For some reason, humans feared her. Elanora smiled at the thought.

"Where is the site the new tourists are going to visit?"

"They didn't say. They just rented some camping gear. They don't even want to stay the night."

"Is Kirra their tour guide?"

"Yes."

"Does she know where they're going?"

"No...I don't think so..."

Eleanor chuckled loud enough for the receptionist to hear. "I dislike it when people try to bluff. And you are such an amateur in that regard. You don't want to make me angry."

"I'm sorry. But I only work at the reception desk. They don't have all of the information here. Why don't you try the manager?"

"Are you challenging me?"

"Oh, no. I'm sorry. I'm just trying to help."

"Good. So keep an eye out for those travelers. My people are watching you. Don't do anything stupid. Just so you know, your baby is currently well-fed and being taken care of. You needn't worry."

She heard a sniffling sound. "Please...he's only two. Don't hurt him."

"Have I told you he's hurt?"

"No, no. I'm sorry."

"So stop asking questions. Do what you're told. As soon as I have the information I need, you'll have your boy back. I don't like children. I don't want any of my own, let alone other people's..."

"Okay, okay. I get it. Please don't hurt him. The tourists are coming back in. I'll see what information I can get from them."

"All right," Elanora grumbled and hung up. She leaned back in her chair and contemplated. She had never been this close to the deciding point of her power. So close she could smell it. She had made a promise to her father, and she would see this through.

Her clan didn't support her because she was the first female alpha they had ever had. She knew they talked behind her back. She had inherited the role from her father and thus hadn't had to go through a challenge. If she was incapable of following through with her role, however—or if she died—then the challenge would be opened to others.

She frowned at the thought. She had dived so deeply into justifying her rightful position in the masculine clan that she had totally overlooked the idea that the clan members weren't just going to sit around and wait for her to prove herself. The strong males in the clan would most likely go out of their way to prove she was incapable of fulfilling her duties. Or they'd find a way to kill her.

She bolted to the door to call for her guards. But instead of the usual scene where a couple of guards and messengers lurked outside waiting for her orders, she found an empty corridor.

"Oh, no," she muttered to herself and strode along the corridor toward the room where they were holding the receptionist's son.

CHAPTER 30

Leon chased the animal. He would normally call it a big cat, but Mya had called it a shapeshifter before, so just to be on the safe side, he wouldn't make any hasty assumptions. He was, however, quite sure it wasn't simply a cat because a cat wouldn't have taken the time to stalk him and then run away. And this cat was too quick. It had disappeared into the woods like a puff of smoke.

Leon heard footsteps behind him. He turned and saw Kirra racing toward him, weapons in hand. *How can a woman run so gracefully while carrying weapons?* he mused but then shook the thought out of his head. He was sure thinking about a woman without knowing her marital status was inappropriate in any civilized society. He did think about Mya all the time, but she wasn't betrothed to anyone in court.

Kirra said something in English. It was too fast for him to understand. But by the tone of her voice, he guessed she wasn't happy he had chased after the animal. In this world, she seemed to be in charge—kind of like a female warrior. He supposed that was why Mya had referred to her as a *guide*. That word sounded authoritative to him.

He smiled and shrugged apologetically as if he was in the wrong. If she could only see him in the Babylonian court, she would be impressed. There, he was in charge!

A few more sentences streamed from her mouth. She seemed to have realized he didn't understand what she was saying, and she had slowed down her speech considerably.

She pointed toward the woods and waggled her finger, suggesting he was not meant to go in. He nodded.

He reached his hand out, wanting to borrow the strange weapon she was holding. She shook her head and said, "Weapon license." She held up the weapon and said, "Gun."

He repeated, "Gun."

She nodded, jabbed a finger into his chest, then pointed at the gun and shook her head again.

He smiled and nodded. She had no idea he was a competent warrior. He shrugged again.

Before they could turn around to go back to the hotel, a couple of low growls came from behind the trees. He swiveled around quickly, knowing what was coming. The two leopards leaped out, both heading in Kirra's direction. She had a weapon, but it wouldn't be enough to deal with two large wild animals, let alone these strange leopards.

Leon pulled his knife and charged toward the one closest to him. He ran underneath the leopard's body on its airborne path and swung his knife upward. He slit open the animal, and it dropped to the ground in blood and gore.

Kirra pulled a smaller gun and fired a dart at the other. She staggered back as the animal still charged, unaffected by the dart.

Leon turned toward her, lifted his knife, and threw it. The knife stabbed into the animal's back, but it still ran straight at Kirra. He pulled his second knife and threw. The second one stopped the animal in its tracks. It paused and turned around to stare at him.

And then the leopard lunged at him. Leon saw Kirra do something with the larger gun, and it made a snapping sound.

The cat's momentum continued to carry it forward even though Kirra had hit it. It clawed its front feet at Leon's chest before dropping to the ground and lying motionless.

Kirra rushed over. She pulled his torn shirt down to his waist and examined the gashes on his chest. He was still standing and felt fine, but he had to admit there was a lot of blood. He frowned as he thought he saw a tear on her face. He didn't quite understand why she cried.

His mind started to cloud. He must be tired. He pointed to his knives, still stuck in the leopard's body. He wanted to go to his weapons, but his ability to move had slowed.

Kirra rushed toward the knives, pulled them out. She tucked them in her belt and then said something—he didn't comprehend what it was—and slid her arm around his waist.

Is she trying to help me walk? He shook his head as his vision started to blur. There was no way he would let a female guide—whatever that meant—help him walk.

"No, thank you. I can walk by myself," he said in Babylonian, but he was sure she understood. She let go of him. He could feel his body sway. *What the hell?*

She said nothing further but wrapped her arm around him and half-walked half-dragged him back toward the camp. He wanted to protest, but his body and mind wouldn't obey.

He saw Mya and Zach hurrying toward them. *Thank God!* Finally, someone who spoke his mother tongue. He rushed toward Mya, towering over her. "Mya, I'm okay. I don't want to go to the infirmary. Don't let Kirra take me."

"Leon, you're injured. You've lost a lot of blood."

"That's...okay. I'm...okay..."

"Listen to me, Leon." She held his shoulders.

"I...I'm listening..." And then he couldn't hear anything else.

CHAPTER 31

Elanora shoved the dagger deep into the chest of a were-leopard messenger. Its dead body turned into a vile lump of blood and gore, its eyes still staring at her, questioning. She shook her head. She still hadn't learned how to control her temper. And she knew that might be her fatal weakness. She crouched next to the dying leopard.

"You're too young to die. But look at this as a good thing. I'm doing you a favor. We're facing extinction. Dying at my hands is a lot better than at the hands of the nasty forces coming for us." She glanced at the door. "Dex, you can come in now," she called out and wiped her bloody hands on a nearby floral tablecloth.

The room darkened a shade when he walked in. It wasn't just the size of him blocking the light from the small window which let in limited sunlight from the thick woods, but also the fact that his body oozed with an aura of darkness. She didn't think he realized it, but she knew. She would never reveal to him that if he ever decided to exercise his innate dark power, he could be stronger than she was.

"He's just a messenger," Dex grumbled.

"I've done him a favor. Darkness is coming for us, and dying at my hand is a mercy."

Dex chuckled. "I've never seen you scared before."

"I'm not scared," she said.

"Don't hiss. It's unattractive. You're a future leader. Behave like one." He approached her and lifted her chin. He looked down at her, allowing his lips to hover an inch above hers. It was both an inch too close and an inch too far.

A corner of her mouth quirked, and she gazed into his deep purple eyes in challenge.

He stared back then let go of her chin. "I cleaned up the mess in the woods. These two idiots attacked the humans there. They deserved to die more than he did." He pointed at the dead leopard on the floor and bent down to pick up the body.

"That's not your job," she growled.

"My job is to clean up your mess. I can only hope your own body isn't going to one day be a part of the mess." He glared at her and began to carry the body out.

"We have a big job coming from Xiilok," Elanora told him. "The Babylonian court sent people to dig up a jar of potion. We're being paid to stop them from doing so."

Dex stopped at the door and slowly turned around. The body of the dead leopard dangled from its position around his shoulders. His eyes grew even darker. "How many times have I told you not to take jobs from Xiilok?"

Frustrated, she waved her arms in the air. "As far as I'm concerned, you are not feeding the clan, Dex!"

"There's better money elsewhere."

"Money is money. There is no *better* money!"

"Is that why you sent them? To have those humans killed?"

She shook her head. "We need to locate the jar first. Then we must stop them from retrieving it. That's the deal. Those idiots almost killed the Babylonians *before* they got to the jar." She slammed her palms on the table. "Damn it! They haven't done a proper job for a long time. I need you on it, Dex."

Dex dropped the leopard to the floor. "I don't kill humans."

"The Babylonians aren't human. They serve the court, the gods, and the goddesses. They're minor deities. And I'm not asking you to kill them. Just don't let them get the jar."

Dex narrowed his eyes. "Is that all?"

She nodded.

He turned to leave.

"Hey! Who's going to take care of the body?"

"It's your mess. Clean it up yourself," he said and kept walking.

"Dickhead!" she cursed, but he had already walked away and didn't hear her. She pulled a tablecloth off a table to wrap the body in. She stared at the cloth, the flower pattern glaring back at her as if she were a naughty child.

She felt a lump in her throat, but she swallowed it down. She shoved the tablecloth on the shelves, deciding not to use it, and dragged the body out by the neck. She could wash the blood smear off her hands. But she didn't know how to clean the bloody tablecloth.

CHAPTER 32

Being in the hospital as a human wasn't easy, especially when she was accompanying a friend who had come from a different civilization, had traveled across dimensions, and spoke a language that could only be translated by Zach's multiversal technology.

Mya was sure Leon's makeup would be human, just like hers, even though they lived in a different world. But that was the problem. Because she was stationed on Earth, she had a human profile so that she could operate as a person with a normal life. But Leon had nothing in this human world.

God, she had never seen him hurt so badly. That thing in the woods had almost torn his chest open. Luckily it didn't rip his heart out, or he wouldn't have made it to the hospital. She knew he was the head of the temple guards, and in his line of work, there was a lot of physical combat. This surely wasn't the first time he had been hurt. But it was the first time she'd seen him this way.

She shook the thought out of her mind. She felt an urge to switch on her deity mode to check to see if Leon survived. But she wouldn't do that. First, she didn't think he wouldn't be on any of her systems because he didn't live in this world. And second— and she feared this the most— she didn't know what she would do if his name did come up on the dead list, the one that listed those she wasn't supposed to save. Just like in Zach's case.

She turned away from the emergency room and saw Kirra's face soaked in tears. Mya had totally forgotten she not only had company but her company was a person oblivious to her magical world. She approached Kirra. "He'll be fine, Kirra. I've known Leon for a long time. He's been injured a lot in his line of work. And he always walked away from it."

Kirra wiped the tears from her face. "It was my fault."

"No, it wasn't. Why would you say that?"

"I should have loaded the rifle. I was careless. I thought I knew that part of the woods."

"It was Leon who chased the cats first, right?"

Kirra shook her head. "It doesn't matter. It's my responsibility. I shouldn't allow anyone to get hurt."

It was all too familiar to Mya. Once upon a time, she, too, thought she was responsible for everyone on her list. She felt as if she was responsible for every single soul she couldn't save. Now here was this young woman, thinking the same thing.

"Listen, Kirra, you can't think about your job this way. It'll eat you up. I care about Leon. He's a dear friend of mine, and I never want him to get hurt. But you can't hold yourself responsible for everyone's fate, especially if they're not looking out for themselves."

Kirra looked at her. More tears rolled down her face. "He was injured because of me."

"No, I just told you—"

"No, you weren't there. He slit the first leopard in half with that little knife of his. He could have handled the second one the same way. But he threw the knives at it instead because it was lunging at me." She gazed into Mya's eyes. "I'm combat trained, Mya. Almost joined the army. I might not know much about combat, but I know he made a conscious decision to let go of his weapon."

Mya found herself speechless. She had forgotten the fact that Leon was doing all of this voluntarily. On the other hand, she was just trying to do her job and get out of debt to Ishtar.

"Mya!"

"Huh?"

"I just asked what Leon does for a living. He seems very skilled."

"Uhh…" She cleared her throat. "Oh, there you are!" she said in a high-pitched voice when she saw Zach come into the corridor. She grabbed at him like a drowning person reaching for a lifebuoy.

"What's up, Mya?" Zach raised an eyebrow.

"Kirra asked what Leon does for a living. Should I tell her he's the head of the temple guard living at the Babylonian court?" she asked between clenched teeth.

Zach smiled. "Come on, you think she couldn't handle that information? How did you handle the fact that I'm part Eudaizian?"

"But I'm a deity. She's human… I don't know how much she is open to this … this …"

Zach laughed. "There is only one way to find out."

She nodded and was about to say something more when the operating room doors swung open. Mya took one look at the doctor and knew it wasn't good news.

"Mya Portman?" the doctor called out.

"Yes, that's me. I'm his emergency contact."

The doctor glanced her up and down.

"What's the situation, doctor?"

"I need to talk to his next of kin. I couldn't find his information in the database."

Mya looked at Zach. Zach tapped the doctor's shoulder. The doctor stepped aside with him. Kirra approached, standing next to Mya. Zach murmured something to the doctor. Quickly, the doctor came back to Mya and Kirra.

"He's lost a lot of blood. And he has a rare blood type. One I can't find a match for in our blood bank. I guess we'll just have to wait this out."

It felt as if someone had pulled the rug out from under her. "What...what do you mean by that?" Mya asked.

The doctor looked at her with compassion. "I stitched him up. The wounds were deep, and he's lost a lot of blood. There's no infection, which is a good sign. He has a very strong physique, which is also good. But losing that much blood and having no replacement is hard, even for a strong man."

"What are his chances, doctor?" Zach asked.

"Are you sure there's no match in the blood bank?" Kirra asked.

"We've done everything we can. Now we have to rely on the patient's strength to pull him through this. I can't even tell you the odds because this is unprecedented."

"What do you mean by unprecedented? You haven't seen anyone injured that bad?" Kirra said, tears streaming down her face.

The doctor looked at Kirra. "I haven't seen anyone injured like that and having lost that much blood even making it to the operation room. I'll keep you informed. He's in the intensive care unit. No visitors allowed." The doctor nodded a goodbye and turned on his heel.

CHAPTER 33

Zach took a drag of his cigarette and looked at the sky reddening in the corner of the hospital yard. Kirra was right—a gigantic dirt storm was coming, and it would be a very bad idea to be in the eye of it. He hadn't smoked a cigarette in a long time. But it wasn't hard for him to drop a poor habit such as smoking because he didn't do it to satisfy a desperate need. He'd never depended on anything or anyone. There was once a time when he had been completely carefree.

It wasn't the matter of taking on new responsibilities and the fact that many lives depended on him that weighed on his shoulders, it was the cause and effect of it all. Each action he took now had subsequent effects—those that were more significant than he cared for.

He had feelings for Mya, strong feelings. Whether or not it was the big "L" word, he did see himself spending the rest of his life with her. Having taken the Sciphil position, and being part Eudaizian, he had taken on his shoulders the lives of millions of citizens whom he had sworn to serve and protect. The simple matter of wanting to be with Mya now had huge consequences.

Mya and Kirra approached, looking distressed. He knew both of them thought they were responsible for what had happened to Leon.

"I didn't know you smoked," Mya said.

"You know now." He smiled at her.

"What did you tell the doctor?" Mya asked.

"I told him Leon is sorting out his legal status. It's in progress, so right now he's an illegal immigrant and not on the government database. I hoped the doctor would have some compassion."

"Looks like he did, but it isn't enough to save him, is it?" Kirra said, tears welling up again in her eyes.

"Crying your eyes out doesn't help, Kirra," Zach said.

"Do you know something that does?" Mya asked.

Zach nodded. He stood up and squashed out his cigarette. "Yes, I have a solution. But first, we need to bet."

"Betting? Like gambling?" Kirra asked.

Zach nodded. "Essentially." He saw Mya narrow her eyes at him. He knew she was familiar with the procedure. For centuries, she had been handling people's destinies the same way—gambling, betting, negotiating with death. She said nothing.

"My solution will save him but will change him forever. And it can only be done before he dies," Zach said.

"Like turning him into a vampire?" Kirra's eyes widened.

"I'm not a vampire if that's what you're thinking, Kirra. But I'm glad you're open to unexplained phenomena. That makes laying this information out a lot easier." He looked at Mya.

She shook her head. "Leon's a soldier. He's strong. He can survive this."

"That's what I'm saying. We're gambling with his life. Are you sure, Mya? If he dies, there's nothing I can do. I can't bring him back from death. And neither can you," Zach said.

She walked back and forth and then whirled around. She looked at him and then Kirra, letting her arms flop down at her sides. "No, I'm not sure." She waved her arms in the air. "Why did I even think about my Goddess? Of course she wouldn't save Leon. She almost ripped his throat out before."

"Goddess?" Kirra asked incredulously.

"Yes, I'm a deity," Mya said and looked straight into Kirra's eyes, confirming her seriousness.

"Oh...all right. Sure. I've read a lot of fantasy novels. If Leon's your friend, Mya, then he must be a deity, too. I get it. Zach isn't a vampire or alien or anything..." Her voice trailed off when she saw the look on Mya's face. "Is he? Zach is an alien?"

Mya glanced at him.

Zach spoke as slowly as possible. "It's a lot more complicated than that, Kirra. But simply speaking, I don't live on Earth anymore. And the place I live now has a solution for Leon. It has a lot to do with science and metaphysics, and trust me, I'm the last person you want an explanation from."

Kirra nodded. "Okay. That's a lot to absorb in one day. But I can take it. As long as there's a solution for Leon."

Zach looked at Mya. She sighed and nodded.

"All right. Do you know how to handle medical equipment?" Zach asked.

Mya shook her head.

"Just enough for first aid. Like needles, securing simple wounds, and connecting drips," Kirra said.

"That's good enough. I don't have enough time to explain to you about the procedure. But in a nutshell, I'm going to wake him for a moment, and Leon has to consent to what he's receiving from me. It's hardly a consent in his condition, but I'll deal with the consequences of that later. Mya, you have to convince him to say yes. Can you do that?"

Mya nodded.

"I need your help with the medical equipment, Kirra. There's a substance I need to inject into his body via the IV after he agrees to it. Can you do that?"

Kirra nodded.

"All right. Then let's go," Zach said.

"Are you sure about this, Zach?" Mya asked.

"I've seen it done before with my own eyes. So yes, I'm sure." He turned and strode into the long hospital corridor.

The energy he was carrying in his body was one of Eudaiz's top secrets—it was part of the making of a Sciphil's power. If Leon betrayed him or the Eudaizian universe, Zach would have to kill Leon before he could leak any of Eudaiz's secrets, or worse, give a sample of the substance to any of Eudaiz's adversaries.

Thinking about their endless list of enemies, Zach shuddered.

CHAPTER 34

Zach and Mya hid in a storage room near the critical care unit. The room was so small and cluttered with equipment that Zach's and Mya's bodies rubbed up against each other.

"Did you really think I wouldn't come back to the Daimon Gate for you?"

"The thought crossed my mind. But you know why I left. Ishtar threatened to kill all the subjects I had saved. That would be thousands of people."

"Hmmm."

"I know my numbers aren't stacking up to yours, but—"

"It's not the numbers, Mya."

"So what's causing that look on your face?"

"What look? I don't pout."

Mya chuckled. "I'd rather you pouted."

Zach sighed. "I just have a lot on my mind. That's all. What's taking Kirra so long?"

"Come on, Zach. I don't know how to disconnect the security monitors. And you can't do it, either. So stop whining."

"I'm not. I just don't like the smell of meds and cleaning products."

The door of the room slid open, and Kirra appeared. "It's done. Let's go before they turn the monitors back on," she whispered.

Zach and Mya rushed out of the room.

The light in the corridor was still on. Apparently, Kirra had disconnected only the security monitors and nothing else.

"Very impressive. How did you do that?" Zach asked while they raced toward Leon's room.

Kirra shrugged. "It's not rocket science. I just unplugged the monitors."

"So what will stop them from plugging them back in?" Mya asked in astonishment.

"Well, I didn't know which one led to Leon's room, so I cut all of the cords. With a very sharp pair of gardening scissors." She grinned wickedly.

"It'll take them a while to replace the security system."

Mya smiled. They entered Leon's room, and their chatter died.

They had been right the whole time regarding the decision to make Leon take Zach's offer. Leon didn't look as if he would make it. His lifeless body lay motionless. The monitor barely registered his pulse. His skin had turned ashen.

Kirra bit back a tear. "All right, what do you need me to do now, Zach?" she asked.

"This is worse than I expected," Zach said. "I've seen Ciaran do this for his brother before. The thing is, Ciaran used his blood to pump the substance that he injected into his brother's body. His brother recovered instantly. The problem we have here is that we don't have the blood to transmit the energy efficiently throughout his body. We'll still do it, but it will diffuse naturally. Don't expect him to be jumping up and down right away. All I can guarantee is that the procedure works. He'll live."

"We have to be out of here ASAP," Mya said.

Zach nodded. "As soon as we finish, we have to smuggle him out of here."

Kirra nodded with determination. "I'm on it. We can get him out of here promptly. Now, tell me what to do, Zach."

"Okay, get the drips ready."

While Kirra rushed around preparing the needle, Zach concentrated. He sent a sound frequency into Leon to wake him. It didn't work. He tried again. And again. Leon stirred and winced. His eyes fluttered.

"Mya!" Zach called out.

Mya sat down next to the bed and angled her face to ensure she was within Leon's vision as soon as he opened his eyes.

Zach sent another sound wave.

Leon winced again and opened his eyes.

"What's his last name?" Zach asked quickly.

"Baal," Mya responded.

Zach switched on the translator in his wrist unit and said, "Leon Baal, I now name you the successor of Sciphil Two of Eudaiz. Do you accept?"

The machine translated what Zach said to Leon. He frowned, and then his eyes almost rolled back. He was going to pass out again.

Mya spoke in Babylonian, and the computer translated back in English. "Leon, you're injured. The only chance you have to survive is to accept what Zach is offering. I understand you have your loyalty to the court. But this is your life. And Ishtar didn't save you when you needed her. Take it. Please."

Leon frowned.

Zach raised an eyebrow but said nothing.

"Leon, please say yes. You took on this mission because of me. If anything happens to you, I'll never forgive myself. You probably don't know what's going on. So if you trust me, just say yes."

"Leon Baal, I now name you the successor of Sciphil Two. Do you accept?" Zach repeated.

Leon glanced at Mya quickly. Zach couldn't see Mya's face, but he saw a tear fall on Leon's face. Leon turned toward him and said, "Yes." Then he passed out again.

"Kirra," Zach called. "Come here, please." He peeled his shirt off. "On my back, on the right-hand side, about six inches from my shoulder, can you see a faint bruise mark?"

"Yes," said Kirra.

"Stick the needle in there and draw out some substance."

"Some? How much?"

"Just fill up the needle cylinder." It might be a little too much, Zach thought, but he didn't have time to check with Eudaiz for the precise dosage. He felt the needle puncture his shoulder, and his most precious energy was drawn out.

For a second, he felt dizzy. "That's enough," he said.

When he turned around, he could see the semitransparent silver liquid nearly filling the cylinder of the syringe. He realized how crucial that energy was, and he now remembered that Sciphil Nine gave Ciaran's brother only a few drops.

Zach pointed at the IV drip. Kirra nodded and darted to the tube. She injected the substance into the tube to transport it throughout Leon's body.

Very shortly, Leon's pulse registered stronger on the monitor. Zach shook his head, trying to stay alert as his vision wavered. "We need to go now," he said.

Mya pushed a wheelchair in. She and Kirra loaded Leon onto the chair. Zach tried to help, but every movement he made was like trying to move mountains.

"Are you okay, Zach?"

He saw Mya's face hovering in front of him. Her image wavered as if it was floating in water.

"Zach!"

"Huh?"

"Are you okay?" Mya asked again.

"I might have let too much of my eudqi be taken out..."

He felt her arm slide around his waist.

"No, I can manage. Let's go."

Mya continued to hang on to him, and he was inwardly thankful. He had a feeling he would be falling and planting his face on the floor if she were not helping him. Kirra pushed the wheelchair. They raced along the corridor. At the far end, the shadows of security officers moved toward them.

"The other way," Mya said and steered Zach in another direction.

They stormed out to the parking lot and loaded Leon into the backseat of the SUV. Kirra quickly folded the wheelchair and threw it in the trunk.

"You're in the backseat, Zach." she said.

"Excuse me?" Zach protested.

Kirra said nothing but just stuffed him into the backseat of the car.

"I'll drive," Kirra said as she strode toward the driver's side. Mya climbed reluctantly into the passenger seat in the front. Their SUV charged out the gate of the hospital at the same time that security rushed out the front door.

Kirra fishtailed into the dirt lot of the campsite. Zach staggered out and went over to the other side to help get Leon into the wheelchair, but Mya and Kirra had beaten him to it.

They had only walked a few feet when they heard low growls from the nearby trees.

"About damn time," Kirra grunted between her teeth and pulled out the rifle in her car, loading it quickly.

"You have to take Leon to the room, Zach. Let's us take care of these animals," Mya said.

Zach didn't like the idea of women protecting him, but he wasn't stupid and irrational. There was no room for egotistic masculinity now. He was weak. Without Eudaizian technology, he'd have to recharge his eudqi naturally. It took time, and he needed to rest.

He raced toward the room with the wheelchair, pushed Leon inside, and slammed the door behind him.

He was exhausted. He knew he should jam the door with something and secure the window. But before he could do anything, he heard a low growl from a dark corner of the room.

CHAPTER 35

Mya took the combat knife Kirra gave her and followed Kirra. For a brief moment, she wondered if Kirra had been put in her file as a case to save or on the list of people destined to die. She shook the thought from her mind. She was on a different mission now, and she was sure her balance didn't count in this case. And that was for the best.

Two men in their late forties walked toward the office from the corner of the yard. They stopped when they spotted Kirra and Mya at the edge of the bush.

"Kirra, what are you doing over there? Is your friend okay? I heard about the accident," one of them said.

Kirra smiled. "He's fine. We just want to make sure everything is good here."

"It's weird that the cats came out of the bush like that. I heard the office call for some professionals to search the area," the other man said.

"What professionals?" Kirra asked.

The man shrugged. "I don't know. I guess it has to do with wildlife preservation or some expert in that regard."

Kirra shrugged. "All right. I'll let them know if there's anything unusual tonight."

The man chuckled. "Don't stay too late, and don't go into the woods."

"All right. We'll just search around the yard." Kirra grinned.

The two men walked away.

Mya turned back to look at Kirra and saw that she had darted into the bush. Cursing, she rushed after her.

***

In the room, a leopard stepped out from the corner. Zach was one hundred percent sure this one wasn't an ordinary leopard. It wasn't even an ordinary shapeshifter—if he could consider shapeshifters to be ordinary creatures. Something about this creature—whatever it was—was magically different.

Zach knew he was in no shape to fight. He could use the gun he brought from Eudaiz—he was sure it could kill space creatures—but it hadn't been tested on magical creatures. If he fired, and the gun didn't work, then he and Leon would end up the leopard's dinner.

At least, at the moment, the animal wasn't attacking. It moved around the bed and approached Zach. It sniffed his hand. It was so close he could smell it—the earthy smell of a wild animal.

"We don't mean you any harm," he said and was sure it understood him. The animal looked at him with haunting green eyes. It licked his hand.

At the other corner of the room, Leon stirred in the wheelchair and started to wake.

Zach cursed silently but said nothing. He felt a tug on his hand. He looked down and saw the leopard was trying to yank his wrist unit off. He jerked his hand away.

It looked up at him and bared its teeth. He thought he saw a flash of an ancient woman's face, but it just as quickly returned to the leopard's face. Maybe he had hallucinated it.

"Whatever you are, I can't let you take my wrist unit."

Zach shuddered, thinking about the consequences of that. The wrist unit not only carried his biological profile but also whatever it was that made him a Sciphil. He'd destroy it before he allowed it to drop into the wrong hands, even if he had to die. Zach stepped back.

A deep voice croaked out from the leopard's mouth, saying, "Magic...the gate...give me..." and then it approached his right hand again. He got the impression that if he jerked away again, it would bite his hand off. So he reached his hand out. The animal sniffed it. *Why does it want to get my wrist unit?* he thought as he slid his left hand under his jacket where he kept his gun holstered.

As fast as he could manage, he pulled the gun and shot the animal. The laser beam hit its fur and absorbed into its skin.

No injury to the animal. Not even a scratch. *Shit!* he thought.

The animal bared its teeth, and Zach stepped back. It leaped at him. He pulled his dagger and stabbed its chest. Surprisingly, the dagger caused some damage, but the momentum and the weight of the animal pushed Zach to the floor.

It withdrew slightly and then charged at him again.

From behind the animal's back, Leon leaped at it with a knife in his hand. He stabbed it in the back, pulling the knife down and almost slicing its back in half. The animal howled in pain and whirled around, throwing Leon to the floor.

Zach jumped up and took his turn, stabbing at the animal's back as it charged at Leon.

The animal had been weakened. In addition, the room was too small for it for gain any more momentum. So when Zach stabbed it, it fell short of landing on Leon. It bit his left leg, and Leon tried to yank it away.

Zach pulled his dagger out and stabbed again.

The leopard swung around quickly. Zach ducked, but it was still able to sink its teeth into his left shoulder. It hurt, but it was a lot better than the cat getting his right shoulder, as that would be too close to his eudqi point. Zach fell and saw stars. On the way down, he stabbed one more time at the leopard's chest.

It roared. He knew it was badly hurt.

He rolled away to avoid it landing on him.

There were footsteps and bangs on the door. Then the door swung open, and the two security men stood in the doorway with guns in their hands. The gun he brought from Eudaiz didn't work before, he wasn't sure the primitive guns on Earth would work. But he had no other choice.

From behind, Zach saw Leon approaching. He sprung quickly to his feet and grabbed at the animal's back. It was heavy. Leon darted forward and grabbed it from the other side. Together, they pushed the animal toward the door where it received several bullets from the security officers.

To Zach's surprise, the earthly technology killed the magical creature.

Zach was sure that was the end of it. He hoped so because that was the end of his energy. His knees buckled, and he heard a thud on the floor before his own body hit it. It must have been Leon.

Lying on the floor, Zach heard a haunting howl from the bush in the distance. It was hollow and eerie. Was it an animal? He thought it might not be an animal cry but one from some kind of magical creature.

He had a feeling they had stirred up something evil, and the day of doom was coming their way.

Then he heard nothing else.

CHAPTER 36

Zach woke to find himself staring at the white ceiling of the small hotel room. Whatever he was lying on was comfortable, so he didn't think he was on the floor. He remembered what happened and immediately reached for his wrist unit. It was still there. He sat up abruptly and saw Mya and Kirra sleeping on the floor in a corner. He was lying on the only bed in the hotel room, and next to him was Leon, who had also sat up and was panting.

"Oh great!" Zach muttered, looking at the women sleeping on the floor, their heads resting on folded hotel towels. He got up and went to the corner.

Leon stood gawking at his chest in the mirror. There wasn't even a faint scar from his wounds.

Zach knew well the confused feeling Leon was experiencing. His eudqi had healed Leon. Zach carried a scar on his chest because the wound he suffered in Eudaiz had been fatal, and the blade that had pierced his heart wasn't an ordinary sword but one belonging to the most notorious monster in the cosmos.

On that scale, a few scratches on Leon's chest didn't compare, even if from a shapeshifter. Zach sat on the floor next to Mya and pulled her up into his arms. He kissed her forehead. "It can't be comfortable sleeping on the floor," he whispered into her ear.

She opened her eyes groggily and smiled at him. "How're you feeling?" she asked.

"Good as new. You know how Eudaizian energy heals me. You've seen it."

She smiled. "Indeed."

Kirra awoke and sat up, leaning against the wall. "This is the weirdest thing I've ever seen in my life," she said.

Zach chuckled. "At least you're open to possibilities."

Leon turned around and pointed to his chest. He mangled out a single English word, "Fixed." Then he grinned.

"You're more than fixed. You're glowing," Kirra said.

"We couldn't have done it without you, Kirra," Zach said. "How did you girls convince security to leave us in here after the leopard stunt?"

"We didn't convince them of anything. They had to dispose of the animal, and we said we'd take you boys to the hospital. Then Kirra just drove around the block and came back."

Zach chuckled. "So you didn't really go into the bush last night, did you?"

Kirra shrugged and said nothing.

"Jesus Christ, Kirra! And I can't believe you let her—" Zach looked at Mya.

Mya cut in, "I couldn't stop her, Zach."

"Not her fault. I have legs. I can go wherever I want," Kirra deadpanned.

"I know you feel responsible for what happened to Leon. But it wasn't your fault. We came here for a reason, and that's what drew the wild animals in," Zach said.

"And living your whole life feeling responsible for others' actions sucks," Mya said. "Luckily the gun discharge scared the cats away. Otherwise, we wouldn't be sitting around here now."

Zach scowled. "Cats. How many were there?"

"Only a couple. But as Mya said, the gunshots scared them away. So yes, you saved the day. Happy?" Kirra stood.

"They weren't scared of the guns. I don't think so." Zach shook his head. "There was something unusual about the cat we killed last night. And I heard a howl, like a mourning cry from the bush."

Kirra nodded. "That must have been from the little cat."

Mya shook her head and sat on a small chair in a corner of the room. "It wasn't a little cat. It was a lynx."

"A what?" Kirra asked.

"Lynx? As in the popular grooming products for men?" Zach asked with a straight face.

Leon sat on the bed. He didn't look happy as he couldn't grasp what the conversation was about.

Mya tied her long hair back, making her face look sharper, her eyes bigger and darker. "The lynx is a kind of wild cat. The magical lynx is extremely dangerous because it has more talent than ordinary cats. I can't imagine what a shapeshifter lynx could do. I thought magical lynxes were extinct."

"How can you be so sure it was magical? It looked like a wild cat to me," Kirra said.

"I've seen it in the Babylonian court. Leon knows it, too, if he can understand what we're talking about here. And in terms of talent, one of the most dangerous tricks a lynx can do is psychic. It can see through solid objects."

They turned and looked at Leon and saw his eyes had darkened. He had made sense of part of the conversation and had speculated the rest. By the look on his face, his speculation might be quite close to the mark.

Zach shook his head. "Now we're talking about a lynx shapeshifter with psychic ability. That explains why, when we killed the cat last night, I heard a shriek from the woods. It seems we didn't kill just any cat but one of importance to the lynx in the woods. We pissed it off. Great!"

Mya stood. "So the cat last night simply paid you a visit? Or did it want something? I imagine if it had wanted to eat you alive, it would have just attacked. There was no point luring us away to get into this hotel room and wait for you."

Zach frowned and looked at his wrist unit. Then he looked at Mya. "It wanted my wrist unit."

"It wanted to wear your watch?" Kirra arched an eyebrow. "I can't imagine it would have a lot of use for that in the bush."

Zach shook his head. "This isn't an ordinary watch. It has a map and a connection to the multiversal gateway. Our wild cats wanted to travel the multiverse. But why? I wonder if it'll come back for the wrist unit."

Kirra stood and headed for the door. "If they come again, I'll have more rifles waiting."

"Don't worry about getting more rifles," Zach said. "I'm afraid they're too slow. My gun can kill most space creatures in the cosmos, but it didn't do the cat last night any damage. It does appear that metal from ordinary earthly objects such as bullets and knives hurt it. You should see what Leon did with his little knife last night."

Zach approached the table in the corner to get to Leon's knife. Before he got there, he heard Leon's objection in English, "Don't touch yourself. Let me."

"Excuse me?" Zach spun around to see Leon had stood up from the bed.

Mya and Kirra rolled out laughing.

Leon frowned at the women's reaction.

Zach turned on his unit's translation function and explained to Leon how people would misunderstand what he had just said. Leon's face looked as if it was on fire, and he sat back down.

Zach chuckled. "I guess your English is still a lot better than when we met a short while ago. I couldn't do any better than that with a foreign language, so don't be too hard on yourself." Then he put on his jacket and headed for the door.

"Mya and I will go to the site today. Given the situation, we'll need more knives," Zach said.

"I know where you can get a lot of combat knives...legally," Kirra said and followed Zach to the door.

"I'll explain to Leon about the Sciphil position and what we did to save him while you're gone. But I'll bet he will want to go to the site, too," Mya said.

"Yes!" Leon said in English and stood. He pointed to his chest. "It's fixed."

Zach approached and lowered his voice. "The one that scratched your chest was a rookie. The one that bit you last night wasn't." He pointed at Leon's leg. Everyone looked. The wound was bleeding, and the blood was dripping down to the floor.

Before anyone asked a question, Zach pointed at his shoulder. "My wound healed because I'm a Sciphil. He's not. He's using my energy just to stay alive. You have a lot to explain to him now, Mya.

We'll get more medical supplies at the store. But he's going nowhere with that leg."

Zach turned and exited the room.

CHAPTER 37

Elanora roared. She had shifted and had no intention of returning to her human form. She whirled around the confined space of her room, knocking everything to the floor as she moved. The two guard creatures standing at the door shook uncontrollably.

How pathetic! she thought. *What a disgrace for generations of leopard shapeshifters!* But she wasn't one of these ordinary were-leopards. She was special. That was why she was destined to be the leader.

She was a lynx. One of the last remaining on Earth.

But whether it was worth it or not, she had no clue. Especially now. She walked around the room. She had kept the furniture at a bare minimum as she didn't see herself being here for long. There was nothing here she felt attached to. She belonged elsewhere. She looked out the tiny window and howled out her frustration and anger.

She was sure the guard leopards were paralyzed with fear. She might as well help them out. She darted to the door as fast as lightning. Before they could react, she had ripped their throats out.

She licked her lips, savoring the taste of fresh blood. She had forgotten how delicious were-leopard blood was.

Suddenly she was knocked sideways, and her head smashed against the wall. She was dazed. She knew only Dex could overpower her—but she had thought he didn't know his strength. She scrambled to all fours and was tackled again by Dex in his human form.

"Shift back," he growled.

She wriggled but couldn't get out of his grip, so she stayed still. "Shift back, or I'll knock you out of your cat form."

She wriggled again then gave in and shifted back to her human form, totally naked. He let go of her. She strode into the room then turned to look at him.

He grabbed some clothes from a cabinet and thrust them at her.

She threw them to the floor.

His eyes darkened. "So you would rather wear this?" He pulled the stained floral tablecloth off the shelf and threw it at her.

She bared her teeth, but before she charged at him, he wagged his finger. "If I wanted to expose your secrets, I would have done so, Elanora."

She let out a low growl but didn't advance on him—mainly because she knew he was a lot stronger than she. Her mind was clogged with rage at the moment, but she knew it would be a stupid move to go head-on with Dex.

"I know you're not a purebred lynx." He paused and gazed into her eyes. "Is it worth living your whole life keeping this stupid secret?"

"Yes!" she snarled and then felt like laughing. It was such a joke fate had played on her. Dex knew her deepest secret. The secret that the only person she cared for had just died to protect. And Dex said it as if he were relaying any piece of mundane information he handled day in and day out in his line of work.

He was a mercenary. She already knew that. And now it turned out he was a spy as well. He had been sent here to watch her every movement.

"I don't believe you," he said patiently.

"I was born to do this, and this is just what I *will* do. Now get out of my sight."

He shook his head. "I come and go as I please. I'm not in your employment. And on that note, your superior, the one who actually employs me, won't be impressed when he finds out you killed his guards simply because you were mad that some old leopard in your clan was killed for trespassing on human territory."

She flew at him, reaching her hands out to claw at his face. He caught them in the air. She growled, "She wasn't just some leopard!"

He spun her around and pushed her against the wall. "You're talented. You want to become a leader. That's fair enough. But you have grabbed the very pointy end of the deal, Elanora. It sucks, don't you think? What kind of life is it when you can't even mourn your mother's death?"

She shoved him away. "You know nothing, Dex. And don't think you're invincible."

"No, in fact, I'm quite vulnerable when it comes to you."

He approached her again, but she shoved him away and bolted for the door, kicking a chair over on her way out. Just outside the door, she remembered the tablecloth, the only thing she had left of her mother. She stormed back in and grabbed it. Dex threw the set of clothes at her again. "Put some clothes on for pity's sake."

"My life. My choice. If you want to expose my secrets to your *employer*, do so. But don't interfere with what I do. Or you'll die before you have a chance to regret it." Then she turned and left the room.

CHAPTER 38

As much as she was eager to get to the site to retrieve the potion, Mya walked a little slower than usual. The bushland path wasn't exactly designed for sprinting. And she didn't want Leon to feel he was slowing everyone down. He was still limping a bit from the wound on his leg, but she couldn't talk him out of this trip. He hadn't come all the way from the court to stay in a hotel room.

The woods became thicker as they walked. It was strange that the air was filled with birds singing rather than the eerie hum and low growl she had heard the other day when chasing the leopards with

Kirra. But this was a different section of the woods. That might explain the difference.

She shifted and felt the weight of the combat knife Zach had equipped her with. She hoped she didn't need to use it. But what had happened in the last few days might prove otherwise.

Zach walked beside her. He had been quiet on the way here. Since he had returned from Eudaiz, she had totally lost the ability to peek into his mind. Not like she ever could do that completely, but she had gotten some fragmented information here and there. Now his mind was like a black well, dead silent and bottomless to her.

"Are you sure this is the only way to the cave?" Zach asked Kirra, who was walking beside Leon.

She arched an eyebrow. "Your technology couldn't provide you with an alternate route after Mother Nature destroyed your one and only path. I don't think you're in a position to question me, Zach. You'll just have to rely on me."

Zach shrugged. "I guess you're right. Thanks for taking the time. As soon as we get there, you might want to head back to camp."

"Sure." She rolled her eyes.

Mya chuckled and said nothing. It dawned on her now that Zach hadn't been in touch with his people in Eudaiz for a few days. He deliberately avoided using his wrist unit, even when he needed it. When he told Kirra the location function on his device had died, Mya knew he was lying. She knew he was trying to prevent the adversaries from getting a connection to the gateway to Eudaiz. She was amazed by the loyalty and attachment Zach had developed with that universe given his short time there.

It must be a wonderful universe to live in. And she was glad she was getting close to going there with him.

Too much distraction, she thought. She had to concentrate and gather up all the possible deity power she had. She wasn't exactly sure how she would summon an object that had never belonged to her, but she always managed to figure things out. The prospect of being free from her debts excited her. She would be able to be with Zach. That was even more exciting. For more than a thousand years, she had never had such a feeling. Was this what humans referred to as happiness? She didn't know what it was, but she knew she wanted it.

Leon had his headphones on, listening to English lessons. He couldn't hear the conversation, but when he saw everyone start to talk, he turned off the iPod Mya had bought him. She was amazed by his ability to adapt to this world. Who would have thought that only a short while ago, he had been the head of the temple guard in the Babylonian court, a civilization that had slipped out of this human dimension.

"What's up?" Leon asked.

"We are nearly there," Kirra said. "Zach was asking if there was an alternate route."

Leon smiled. "He's scared."

"Excuse me!" Zach turned and looked at Leon.

He chuckled. "I'm sorry. I meant you *care*."

Zach glared at Leon and turned to look ahead. Leon winked at Kirra.

"I know what you're up to, Leon," Zach muttered without looking back. "You're my successor. It's like being an apprentice. Keep that up, and you'll see if I can do you some damage."

"Are you going to whip him?" Kirra asked and laughed.

Before Zach said anything further, the path opened to a wider and clearer area in the middle of the deep woods. There, he recognized the site. His wrist unit beeped softly.

"We're here," Mya said. It was more to confirm it to herself than in question. A tingling sensation ran through her body. She could feel it—an urge to discharge her energy through her fingertips. She had never had that feeling before. Even when she was in her deity mode, this ability rarely came to her.

In front of them, the ground rumbled. A crack ran in a circle, and the ground started to split. It felt like a mild earthquake. As Zach pulled Mya back, Leon pushed Kirra behind him protectively despite her protests.

The encircled area crumbled away, opening up a hole in the ground. When the ground settled, Mya approached the edge of the hole. Zach pulled her back.

"Let me check first," he said and turned his wrist unit on. He located something on the map. He seemed pleased with what he saw. Then he approached the edge of the hole, pressing his foot on the surrounding earth to ensure it was firm enough to stand on. He turned toward Mya. "It's the right place. How do you plan to..." His voice trailed off when he saw her face.

What was wrong with her? Mya didn't know. But the tingling sensation was exploding inside her body and her mind. She thought she might burst into flames at any moment. No words passed her lips. *Okay, control it*, she told herself and tried to calm down. This might be a new ability given to her as guardian of this potion. A new ability so she could summon it.

She focused. In her mind's eye, she gathered the raging source of energy into thin streams of light, weaved them into balls, and pushed them into her right palm. To her amazement, the energy obeyed her. It continued to gather as balls of light in her palm. She smiled at Zach. She knew what to do now.

She approached the edge of the well and reached her palm out. She could feel a suction from her palm to the well. Something was down there. She could feel it. Strong. Powerful. But it was being pulled by her suction and was about to float up.

Then she heard a roar. She turned and saw a leopard fly through the air at her. Its front legs shoved at her chest, pushing her into the well.

CHAPTER 39

Mya was dangling at the mouth of the well by Zach's grasp. His body lay right at the edge of the gaping hole. He grabbed at a tree root with one hand and grasped her hand tightly with his other. If his body slipped into the well, she knew the tree root wouldn't be able to bear the weight of their two bodies together.

Mya heard fighting sounds coming from Leon and Kirra mixed with the animal's roars and growls. She tried to find footing on the wall of the well to ease her weight on Zach, but she had no luck. Her body continued to dangle. And the more she tried to reach her feet to the wall, the more her body swung.

She looked down, and all she saw was darkness. She could not see the bottom of the well, and she was sure she didn't want to be dropped down there. It seemed like Hell's gate. She swore she heard the hum of the devil from down below.

She tried harder to get her footing. Her body swung harder, and she felt the slight slip of Zach's hand. If she kept doing this, he would drop down as well.

Before she looked back up to Zach, she saw a faint red spark from below her. As she breathed in the heated air that drifted upward past her, a thin stream of freezing air brushed over her skin. *So is it hot or cold down there? Is it the bottom of a well or a gateway to something else?* she thought, confused.

"Use your knife," Zach shouted.

She pulled out her knife and stabbed it into the side wall then angled her body and inched up. As soon as her weight eased up a bit, Zach pulled hard. In a quick motion, he hauled half of her body up over the mouth of the well.

There, Mya saw two dead leopards on the ground. Leon and Kirra were bleeding but still standing. Zach pulled her up and away from the well. Leon checked Kirra's injuries. She had a big gash on her arm, and he had suffered a bite wound to one shoulder.

"Are you okay?" Zach asked Mya. She nodded. Zach rushed toward his bag for the medical kit. "Come here, you two." He gestured to Kirra and Leon. Mya ran over to help Zach attend to their wounds, but before they could do anything, a low growl came from the bush.

A magnificent animal walked out from the thick woods. It had the body of a leopard with short brownish hair and a scattering of black spots on its back. But its face was a mixture of wild cat and fox. It had pointy ears with longer fur around the outside of the ears toward the tips.

Its eyes were haunting.

"That's the cat we saw in the bush," Kirra muttered.

"But it's not a cat. Isn't that what you said, Mya?" Zach asked.

"No, it's not an ordinary cat. It's a lynx," Mya muttered.

The lynx paced back and forth in front of them. It glanced toward the well. Then it looked back at them as if choosing which of them it would have for an appetizer and who would be the entrée, side dish, and dessert.

Then it stopped and sniffed the ground. It bared its teeth and charged. From behind them, Leon pushed forward. He did what he had done before in the bush with Kirra. He ran under the flying path of the animal and swung his knife upward. The knife cut into the cat's belly but didn't open it as it had with the other cat. The cat dropped to the ground.

Zach, Mya, and Kirra charged at the injured animal. It quickly scrambled up onto all fours. Although injured, the lynx was still formidable. It tried to leap at them again but only made it a short distance before flopping to the ground.

Zach hurried over to the cat to finish it off, but before he reached it, he saw the shadow of something big jumping out from behind the tree. The front legs of the animal shoved Zach backward, and he fell to the ground. His shoulder bled profusely from the scratch of the animal's claws.

In front of them was something that looked like the king of all leopards. Its gigantic size and dark black fur weren't what made it seem like a symbol of darkness, but rather the aura that emanated from it. Its bright green eyes glared at Zach for a moment, and then it turned and grabbed the lynx by the crook of its neck. Carrying the animal as if it were a fragile toy, it ran into the woods.

Mya ran over to Zach and helped him up from the ground.

"I'm okay," he said. "Let's get the potion and get the hell out of here."

"But you're bleeding. Let me secure your wound first," she said.

"No—we need to get the potion first." He shrugged himself out of her arms and headed toward the well.

She frowned, staring at his back as he walked away. Zach had been really odd since they'd gotten here. She shook the thought away. "Are you okay, Leon?" she asked.

He nodded.

"Kirra?" she asked.

Kirra nodded.

At the edge of the well, Zach crouched and looked down. His soft green eyes darkened. All right, she decided, she was going to try to peek into his mind. She concentrated but saw nothing. *Damn!*

She approached the well, stood at the edge of the hole, and reached her hand out. She concentrated and felt the warmth of glowing energy in her palm. From the bottom of the well, something floated up. It was quite a distance away, and she couldn't tell what the object was, but she guessed it was the potion jar she was supposed to retrieve.

The air seemed to thicken around her. She drew harder, and the object floated up a little more. When her entire body and mind were opened to the energy and her deity ability, she saw sparks of light. In her mind's eye, she saw the whirls of stars. She felt the weightlessness of the empty space in her mind. It was strange. It was different. But it was powerful.

Then she had a vision that explained why Zach had pushed for her to retrieve the potion.

She opened her eyes, and the glow of energy around her and her hand dissipated. A few feet below her was the little jar of potion, hovering in the air.

It stopped rising from the well as her energy winked out.

CHAPTER 40

Mya turned to look at Zach, and he looked about to burst into flames.

"What's up, Mya?" he asked, his eyes still glued to the hovering jar.

"You used me!" She swallowed the lump in her throat. She hadn't let the jar drop back down just yet, but she would.

"What?" he exclaimed.

From behind, Leon and Kirra approached. "What's going on?" Kirra asked.

A tear rolled down Mya's cheek. "Ayana died to save you. You want that jar to bring her back—at any cost."

"No..." Zach started. "Okay, yes. I need that jar. You do, too, because it will pay off all of your debts. Please don't drop it, Mya."

More tears streamed down her face. "Now you're lying to me."

"I'm not lying."

"That's not the real reason you want the jar."

"It is. But it's not the only reason. I'm telling you the truth. Please don't drop it. May people will die if you do. Please don't—"

"But many will also die if I don't let it fall back into the well. I can see it. I can see them dead because of me."

"They're bad people. Xiiloks are bad news, Mya."

"Who are you to say, Zach? All creatures are equal. All universes are equal..."

"You're too naive, Mya. There is nothing equal in the multiverse. All creatures compete for survival. They all take advantage of the one another... Please don't drop the jar, Mya."

She looked down. She could see the bottom of the well now. It was no longer black but a whirl of blue and white light. It was indeed a gateway. In her vision, she had seen the balance of her file if she executed this mission. Drawing the energy from the well would open the gateway and suck the energy out of the Xiilok's well—that universe's life force.

Zach continued, "Creatures in Xiiloks are bad, Mya. They are the outlaws of the multiverse. If you don't do this now, we will never have another chance to destroy that universe. They have killed millions of citizens in Eudaiz, Mya."

"I've never been to either of the universes. I don't know who is good and who is evil. I can't make that decision. There are innocents living in Xiilok. I don't care what they once did. They have redeemed themselves and have chosen to live there. If I do this, they'll end up on my deity dead list. I can't have that on my conscience, Zach."

"Can you have the deaths of millions of Eudaizians on your conscience? If you let go of a few thousand, I will take you to Eudaiz. We will negotiate with Ishtar, and you won't have to pay that debt."

"I don't work that way, Zach. I don't count innocent souls that way." She still held her hand over the well. The energy flow was on hold, and the jar still hovered. "I'm sorry, but I have to let this go, Zach." She turned her palm.

"No!" Zach flew over to the well and let himself free fall. He hovered in the pool of energy, just above the jar.

Kirra squealed and tried to grab him, but he was just out of her reach. "Please don't let go, Mya!"

Kirra cried out. Leon pulled Kirra back from the edge. He understood what was going on. But he was experienced enough to know that he should not interfere with Mya right now.

Mya's hand shook. Zach looked up at her. His soft green eyes were full of challenge. If she let the jar go, he'd go with it. But by bringing it up, she was sure she would kill thousands. The millions of Eudaizians Zach claimed would die were not on her files, so she didn't know how accurate that was. And now she was faced with choosing between him or the thousands of Xiilok people.

More tears rolled down her face.

"Please don't let go. Pull him up, Mya," Kirra cried, kicking her legs and trying to wriggle free from Leon's grasp.

Zach said nothing. He just looked at Mya.

Her hand shook again. She had no idea what to do. She wiped tears away with her free hand as she made her decision. But before she could execute it, the whirlpool at the bottom of the well suddenly vanished.

The energy was vacuumed out of the well. The jar dropped into nothingness. And Zach followed.

Mya could see that her hand looked again like a normal human hand—with no power whatsoever.

CHAPTER 41

She must have screamed, and the sound she made stopped Kirra from squealing. She flopped down at the edge of the well. She was sure she would see either the dark bottom of the well that had sucked Zach down to Hell's gate or his dead body sprawling on the ground. Neither was something she wanted to see. But to her delirious surprise, Zach clung to the wall of the well, jabbing his dagger into the wall for purchase with one hand and, with the other, gripping the uneven surface and working his way up.

"Rope!" Kirra shouted and darted to her camping bag. She pulled out a roll and wrapped it around a tree trunk then threw the rest down the well. Every movement she made was artistic and precise, coming from years of experience in the camping business. Mya jumped out of her way.

In the well, Zach grabbed the rope. Leon helped Kirra, and the two of them pulled Zach back up. Soon he was back up to the mouth of the well.

Mya was sure he deliberately avoided looking at her. He thanked Kirra and Leon then made a beeline toward his bag. "I have to go back to Eudaiz now." Then he looked at Leon. "I appointed you as my successor just to save you. You're a good soldier, and it would be an honor to have you. But I imagine you'd like to go back to your court. If you don't want to go with me, consider this offer lapsed."

Leon said nothing.

Zach continued. "There is one thing I have to ask of you. The energy I put into your body will be there for a while. I'll check with Eudaiz about how long it will last and how to erase it from your system without harming you. But until we can do that, be careful. If our adversaries capture you, we'll have to kill you before they can get a sample of your energy."

Mya approached and touched his shoulder lightly. "You're still bleeding. Let me—" He shrugged his shoulder out from under her hand and walked away.

"His heart bleeds a lot more, and I doubt that wound will ever heal," Kirra mumbled loud enough for Mya to hear.

Mya felt more tears running down her face. *Come on, big girl, you can handle this*, she told herself. She wiped her tears and turned to her bag.

"Zach!" Leon called out.

Zach stopped walking. But before he went to Leon, he crouched next to Mya. She stuffed random things from the ground into her bag. She didn't even know what she was grabbing—she might have stuffed tree branches and rocks into the bag for all she knew.

Now it was her turn to not look at him. But he tilted her chin up and looked into her eyes. His soft green eyes had returned to their usual gentleness. "I just want to let you know I don't regret my feelings for you. What we had together was beautiful. I treasure it and will never forget it. I'm sorry we can't resolve our differences and it has to end this way."

He wiped a tear rolling down her face with his thumb.

"I hate to see you cry. You are a good deity, and your actions are always just. Don't let anyone tell you otherwise."

His wrist unit beeped. He glanced at it. He read the message and then smiled. "Eudaiz has stopped the plot. Nobody will die now. That's a load off."

"Can you tell us exactly what just happened?" Kirra asked. Don't you think we deserve to know? Look, we just saved your ass." She pointed toward the well as a reminder.

Zach nodded. "Yes, you did. And I'm grateful. Simply speaking, there's a scar in the multiversal system that was supposed to be fixed—but nobody fixed it. It's like a wormhole that connects the well in Xiilok and this one. If the energy is sucked up from this well, it drains the Xiilok well and destroys that universe. The evil guy in Xiilok had been doing his best to stop that connection."

"Well, to me, he sounds like a good guy trying to save his universe," Kirra muttered.

Zach shook his head. "You don't know what he did and how many people he's killed, Kirra. He saved Xiilok only because it's his last stop and he wants to rule it. No other universe will accept him. He's desperate and extremely dangerous. If he gains power, other universes—including Earth—will be in very deep shit, to speak in layman's terms."

Kirra shrugged.

Zach continued, "He didn't want to fix the broken wormhole. He wanted to locate it, break it himself, and connect the other end point to Eudaiz instead of Xiilok. He wants to blow a few million people up. He isn't a good guy and isn't kind to anyone, let me assure you of that, Kirra."

"Roger that," Kirra said and grinned.

"We have a wicked king. You'll like him if you get to meet him. He shot down the reconnection and got the jar as well. We missed the chance to destroy Xiilok, but we'll get them sooner or later. Our king said he'll give the jar to Ishtar, and that will absolve Mya of her debts."

Mya stood and looked at Zach.

He looked back at her. "You should be happy, Mya." He nodded a goodbye to everyone and turned around.

"Zach," Leon called again.

Mya guessed Leon wanted to be a successor and travel with Zach to Eudaiz. She swung her heavy bag on her shoulders and walked away.

CHAPTER 42

Zach watched Mya's back as she walked away. He meant what he had said to her. He would never forget those moments they had together. He wondered if she understood that. He wondered what the pecking order of love and feelings was in her righteous deity mind. What good could it be for her to live a life like that? It was hard to believe she had been living that life for more than a thousand years.

When she'd hesitated to trade his life for the thousands of those strangers she wanted to save, he had understood the reason, but it still hurt. He couldn't believe it hurt so much in that short moment of time. He knew it was his fault for putting her—and himself—through it. But he was a man on a mission. And she was a woman who always lived up to the responsibilities of her duty. There was nothing he could do to resolve their differences.

"What's that Leon? You want to go with me to Eudaiz?" he asked absently, his mind still wandering after Mya.

Leon opened his palm and showed him something that looked like a badge.

Zach looked at it and shrugged. "What's this?"

"It's Mya's."

"So she forgot it? Why don't you give it to her?"

Leon shook his head and tried to find the words to explain. Zach reached to his wrist unit to turn the translation device on, but Leon gestured him to stop.

"I'll say this in your language, Zach. Once and for all. Mya had decided to let you drop to the bottom of the well."

Zach merely nodded. The pain had become so unbearable that he couldn't say a word.

Before, it had been speculation and uncertainty. But now, it was a fact that she had decided not to save him in order to save the lives of strangers. She would have let him die, just like that.

He inhaled and shoved his hands in his pockets, waiting for Leon to finish what he was saying.

"Mya dropped this badge to the ground intentionally because she wanted me to have it."

"Meaning?"

"It means she would jump in after you."

"She..." He couldn't find the words. He dropped his bag to the ground. "She..." he repeated but couldn't put the sentence together.

Leon continued, "Transferring the badge means she relinquished her duty as a deity—while she was in debt and on an incomplete mission. It is the biggest disgrace. It negates all of her achievements over a thousand years. She would be condemned after she died with you at the bottom of that black hole."

"She..." Zach had tried for the third time to put a sentence together without success. He shifted his weight back and forth from one foot to the other, not knowing what to do.

Kirra approached and pointed. "She went that way."

Zach nodded. "Thank you, he said and darted in the direction Kirra had just pointed.

CHAPTER 43

Mya stopped at the fork of the path. Her sense of direction wasn't poor, but she had absolutely no idea which road to take now. She dropped her heavy bag to the ground. She unzipped it and found that she had indeed stuffed a couple of rocks in with her other things. She took them out. Then she took more things out. She flopped to the ground and started crying. She heard footsteps. It must be Leon. Wiping her tears away, she waited.

From the woods, Zach stormed out. He said nothing but scooped her up from the ground and held her tightly in his arms. She couldn't see his face, but she could feel every ounce of muscle in his body shuddering with emotion. He held her for a long time then released her.

He tilted her chin up and looked into her eyes. "Will you marry me?"

"What?"

"Be my wife. Be with me..."

Before she could say anything, his mouth was on hers. To her, there was no power in this universe or in the multiverse that could compare to his kiss. He pressed her against the tree and ravished her lips. His hands roamed everywhere on her body.

She returned the pleasure in equal measure.

Soon, they would forget the world they were in at the moment.

***

They heard a gentle clapping sound. From behind a tree, a stunning woman walked out. Blood smeared the midsection of her blouse. "I admire you two." She smiled. "I'm Elanora, and I come here in peace."

Mya narrowed her eyes. "You're that lynx."

Elanora laughed. "You're a smart deity. It would be wise to cooperate with me to avoid being hurt."

"You mean to avoid *you* being hurt? I dislike violence against women. But if you threaten my fiancée—"

"What?" Mya asked from between her teeth.

"You didn't have to say anything. I know it was a yes to my proposal."

Elanora rolled her eyes. "I have no patience for your romance. I have to borrow you, Zach. I want only your wrist unit, but I know it won't work without you."

"What makes you think I'd go with you like a meek dog?"

She pulled out a gun and pointed it at him. "This is the reason."

He chuckled.

Mya knew ordinary bullets wouldn't hurt Zach because he was a Sciphil. She was sure this lynx would know that, too. So why was she pointing a gun at him? Then it dawned on her that the gun might be a distraction.

The woman smirked and swung the gun quickly to Mya. Mya dodged, but Zach instinctively jumped over to cover her, turning his back to the woman in doing so. Mya knew what the woman would do, but it was too late for her to do anything.

One of the lynx's precious talents was her psychic ability. This woman had peeked into Zach's mind, and she knew Zach would try to avoid being hit on the eudqi point on the right side of his back when he fought.

Mya shoved Zach hard so that he staggered backward. But the woman's pointy heel still caught Zach's back just below his right shoulder when she swung a kick at him. He was instantly dazed and fell over on to Mya. They both toppled to the ground.

The woman darted forward with the intention of pulling Zach up and holding him captive.

Mya lay on the ground underneath Zach. Elanora bent over to grab him. Mya waited for the right moment then grabbed Zach's dagger, which had fallen to the ground. She arced upward with the blade and hit the woman's midsection. She drew the dagger out and stabbed again.

The woman howled as blood poured out from her wounds. She staggered back then fled the scene before Mya could get up cause more damage.

Mya had no intention to give chase. She turned Zach over, laying him on the ground on his back. He was totally out of it.

"Zach, look at me. Open your eyes for me." She shook his shoulders gently. She knew being struck close to his eudqi point would daze him for hours. He opened his eyes groggily.

"There you are." She kissed his cheek.

He snapped back to reality, and his body tensed up as he tried to reach for his wrist unit.

"Easy, easy now. It's still there." She smiled at him.

"Where's the woman?"

"She took off."

"You chased her off?"

"Impressed?"

He smiled. "Yes. I'm impressed. I can definitely get you a job in Eudaiz."

"I have two pieces of advice for you, Zach. First, don't ever mention your fatal spot. Don't even think about it in your mind. It's more than likely you'll run into mind readers in the multiverse, and you don't want to make it too easy for them. Second, never ever turn your back on a woman like that."

"A woman like what? Beautiful?"

"Lethal."

"Yes, Professor Portman."

"You know I don't like when you to call me that, right?"

"It's the last time I'll call you by that last name."

"Hey, I haven't promised you anything."

"Yes, you did—in your mind. I'm psychic."

"No, you're not." She pinched him.

"Ouch. Can't you see I'm injured? This isn't helping my recovery at all."

She pinched his arm once more. He winced.

Then they heard a bloodcurdling scream from Kirra. Zach tried to sit up, but he flopped down, useless.

"Don't move."

"Go to Kirra."

"I can't leave you here alone." Mya turned in the direction of the scream and shouted, "We're here!"

Soon after, Kirra rushed toward them. She had a new gash on her arm and was almost out of breath. "It got Leon."

"What is *it*?" Mya asked.

"Are you okay, Zach?" Kirra's eyes zeroed in on Zach.

"Yes, but I can't move yet. What happened to Leon?"

She braced her hands on her knees to catch some breath. "The big black cat. It came back. It did what the brown lynx did. We thought it was sniffing the ground, but it wasn't. It was actually sniffing Leon's blood on the ground. Then it jumped at us. It was incredibly strong. It knocked me out and got Leon."

"Leon seemed able to handle these cats before. Why couldn't he get this one?" Zach asked.

Kirra shook her head. "I don't know. The black cat was very different. It was incredibly strong. But it wasn't just its strength—it bit Leon, and he seemed to be paralyzed from the bite."

"Do you know what kind of cat it was, Mya?" Zach asked.

She shook her head. Zach tried to sit up again, and this time, he was successful with Mya's help. Then he stood. The trio looked toward the wooded area where Leon might have been taken.

As the misty air seeped up from the ground covered by leaves and tree branches, they heard a howling and keening from the magical creatures beyond the treeline.

End of Book 1

BONUS SHORT STORY >>> NEXT

BONUS
SHORT STORY

THE STOLEN

The muffled scream of a child cut through the darkness.

His silhouette shook as he tried to wriggle free of the hands wrapped around his neck belonging to a large man looming over him.

One twist of the hands and the fragile bone of the child's neck would be savaged.

In a single second, everything would end for the boy.

Flash.

His fury had wings. It moved as fast as light and it killed without mercy, without discrimination.

All he had to do was free it.

Today was the day he was born thirty years ago. Tonight was the night he had to kill a man to save a child.

All he had to do was to free it; his Daimon.

His father was philosophical about the Daimon. It was a spirit that was supposed to keep one righteous. But his was violent. There was nothing philosophical about violence, righteous or not.

A kill was a kill.

It was beyond reason. At least that was his father's ideology.

Thing was, his father was no longer with him. Even if his father looked down from Heaven, if there was such a place, and didn't approve of his action; there was nothing his father could do about it. More importantly, he was not to live for anyone's approval. He was his own self and he was the most independent child his father had ever trained.

Independence was the first lesson his father gave him. Since he was two, his father had home-schooled and trained him to make the most of his potential. At five, his physics and his intellect excelled. And at the same time, his father discovered that his talent came with a package: violence.

The talent and the violence made the whole of him. Together, they formed his Daimon.

To his father's expectations, he had learned to utilize his intellect and had suppressed his fury. But he had never promised not to try his fury, to see what it offered. His father had said, too many times, that he was a normal human being. Well, if he was to believe that, he could just be a normal child for once; naughty and curious.

And he saw what his fury did.

When he sent out a flash of his fury, he chopped down ten old trees to the root in one swift hit. The trees Father had been talking about calling in bulldozers to clear the path to the hill, but never found time to do so.

The morning his father told him that a weird storm during the night had conveniently cleared the little bush in their backyard, he'd said nothing. What could a four year old child do with such 'catastrophe'?

He never let his fury out since then. For the most part, when he feared it was getting out of control, he took it out physically on inanimate objects. His furniture hated him.

He got better over the years and learned more of how to control it to a certain extent. One thing had become clear, his fury was not psychological nor was it philosophical; it was primal. It was a beast and it lived in his blood.

He inched closer into the tunnel and the silhouettes had become more prominent, printing against the background of a fast-moving train. The noise of the train covered the scream of the child, and was why only his mind heard the child, and no one else. One second and it would be all over. He could send out his fury right now and save the child.

But, his fury would decapitate the man in front of the child.

Which was worse, dead or witness a decapitation and have blood and gore rain on him? He couldn't speak for the child.

He took over his father's corporate world when he was a teenager; and he was a predator in the business. His intellect was his lethal weapon;

and he had not run into any opponents he couldn't defeat. At the same time, although he hadn't spent a day on the street struggling to make a living, nothing about human behavior surprised him. That was his basic training.

Artificial intelligence, computer science, biology, psychology, chemistry, astrology and the like. They were his toys when he was a kid.

His father swore to him that he was normal!

But now, in front of him was an extraordinary situation of two ordinary human beings. Beneath the obvious size differences of the people in conflict, the silhouettes gave him no additional information. Who was in danger here? The child? The man? Or himself? What if this was a trap to lure him into the tunnel?

He thought he found his soul mate. She understood him and his Daimon. She understood him and his ambition to change life and the landscape of science. She understood his pain. She thrived to make him happy and it had cost her life. She died making him a present for this thirtieth birthday.

Today.

Before he ran himself to the ground with guilt, he found evidence for all the objections to their marriage. He wouldn't label it the way people did, betrayal. It couldn't be a betrayal if she didn't promise him her loyalty first. They loved each other, of that, he was sure. He was even surer that he loved her.

He had run on empty for a few weeks as the world blurred by. He had a responsibility. He had people who depended on him. He had to keep going.

Today, the meeting in freezing winter in New York was a good break from his London office – a place full of painful memories. But as soon as the meeting finished, he circled back to his empty self. He didn't know where his Daimon was, but he was sure a large part of his soul was missing.

His assistant all but begged him not to go for a walk in the snow.

And here he was, standing in front of a tunnel. At the other end were the silhouettes of two people, one of whom he should kill to save the other.

All he had to do was to let his Daimon free.

One second. That was enough time to send out his fury and kill the man. It wasn't the killing decision he was hesitant about; it was who actually needed his help. He stepped further into the tunnel and yelled, "Stop!"

It wasn't the authority or the meaning of the word that stopped the man. It was the intention behind it. The intention to follow suit if the command was not obeyed. The intention to cause harm if necessary.

The man dropped the kid down to his feet.

He had walked halfway through the dark tunnel. Dim light flickered from the other end. He recalled the horror in his assistant's eyes when he said he wanted to go for a walk by himself at this hour in an unsavory part of New York.

"Who the fuck do you think you are?" the man grunted out the words.

He was only a few feet away. It wasn't the man he wanted to see, he needed to see the child. He needed to look into the child's eyes and be certain he had made the right decision.

"This ain't your fucking business. Hear me?"

He kept walking toward the child and the man. The child let out a little moan as the man lifted him up a few inches from the ground, still holding the collar of his shirt. The moan earned the child a slap in the head.

"Stop! Don't make me hurt you," he warned.

He was close enough and he could see the child's eyes now; frightened.

The man kept hitting the boy. "He's mine. I can do whatever I want to him."

There was no need to send his fury out now. He was close enough to break the man's neck with his hands.

"Let the kid go," he said.

"You're a fucking idiot. He had to earn his keep. I can't feed him forever." The man grabbed the kid and dragged him away.

"Leave the kid," he said.

The man stopped, turned around, dropped the child, mumbled some profanity and charged at him. In the dim light, he saw the reflection of a knife. He sidestepped the approach. In one swift move, the man landed on his back, still gripping the knife. The man jumped up to his feet and lunged at him again.

The man didn't give him a choice.

Years of combat training weren't wasted on him. He actually liked it for the most part. The power of body and mind control and what the human body could achieve with the appropriate manipulation of movement always fascinated him. He blocked the second attack, and before the man could thrust the knife at him for the third time, the man's knife had pierced his own throat.

Blood spurted, splattered on him and the child. The man slumped to the ground.

Dead.

He turned and looked at the child. The big brown eyes filled with tears, his small shoulders shook with fear as he stared down at the body of the man on the ground. But he didn't run.

"What's your name?"

The child blinked. "Little Mike."

"That's not your real name."

"Michael Fraser."

He smiled. "That's a lot better. Who's this man, Michael?"

"My stepfather." Michael frowned and played with the hem of his jumper.

"Why did he try to hurt you?"

"He didn't try. He just hurt me." Michael was still examining the hem of his jumper.

He lifted Michael's chin up and looked into his eyes. "Where are your parents?"

"I've never met my father. Mom died last year."

"How old are you?"

"Eight. I don't go to school, if that's your next question." Michael stared straight up at him and didn't go back to the hem of his jumper.

"Do you understand what I just did to your stepfather and why?"

Michael nodded. "He hurt me. You told him to stop but he didn't. He tried to do you with the knife, but he copped that knife in the end. He deserves it."

A cold breeze blasted his face. It wasn't the chill of New York's winter, but the tenacious tone and meaning of what Michael had said that stunned him.

He now understood how his father felt when he made his first explosive compound and blew off the head of the Goddess of Kindness statue in their backyard. His father knew about the fury, the violence; but it was the first time reality dawned on his father that, regardless of how much his son could control himself, the violence would take the better part of him.

His father was devastated; he knew it now, twenty five years later.

He looked at Michael. "Nobody deserves to die, and no one has the right to murder."

"If you didn't kill him, he'd have killed you. Then he'd have killed me. Who would say he doesn't have the right to murder if we had both died?"

"Michael, I killed him in self-defense. That's a totally different matter. But I provoked him first. I did that because I know I can protect myself. What did you do to provoke him, knowing you can't protect yourself?"

"I told him I'd kill him sooner or later."

When he saw the grimace filling Michael's face, a chill crept into his blood. He mentally took a step back from the child. "How did you plan to do that?"

"I ain't have no planning. That was before. But I know now. If I have to kill someone, it will be in self-defense."

He crouched so his eyes were level with Michael's. "Self-defense is not a trick to get away with murder. I don't want to be the one to put that idea into your head. Perhaps, you're too young to understand, but I need to ..."

"I'm not too young. I'm eight years old. I know the most important thing a man gotta do, is to keep his promises. I keep my promises. If he didn't know how to keep his promises, he didn't deserve to live," Michael raised his voice and pointed at the dead man's body.

"Yes, Michael. Keeping promises is very important. But it's not how you judge whether a person deserves to live. In fact, you don't have the right to judge whether anyone deserves to live or die."

"So who will have a say for Nick? He got killed and he has no say. It's unfair. Nick just wanted to protect me. Just like what you did. You can defend yourself, but Nick can't. Nick wanted him to get his hands off of me and ... he killed Nick for that ...he promised my mom he'd care for us... he never did... all he did was hurt me ..." Michael's lips trembled, his shoulders shook with the chill and the emotions, tears filled his eyes but he refused to let them fall.

"Who's Nick?"

"My friend. My only friend. He's the one who made the money, keep the food coming in. But he's still not happy. He wanted more!" Michael pointed at his stepfather.

He could feel his blood boiling. "He killed a kid for not making him enough money?"

Tears started falling down Michael's face. "He shouldn't have bitten him ... I can take a few slaps and punches. I can take it, I told Nick that, but he wouldn't listen. He kept biting and barking until he turned around and broke his neck ..."

"Barking? Is Nick a dog?"

Michael hitched up, almost choking with his tears. "... Yes... his mom died, so my mom brought him home when I was little. He grew up fast and when I didn't have enough warm clothes last winter, he lied on top of me like a blanket."

He reached out a hand to wipe the tears on Michael's face, but the child backed up.

"He made Nick do all the tricks on the road to distract people so I can pick pockets ... days after days, nights after nights ... we were freezing, no food, no warm clothes, but we brought home the money. I promised Nick when we save enough money, I'll run and I'll take him with me. But we don't have enough yet..."

Michael shivered. His jumper was obviously not enough to keep the chill off him. He reached out to Michael, but the child once more backed out. Tears still streamed down Michael's face regardless how many times he wiped.

"We tried. But it's winter. People won't get out that much. We couldn't get much money. He cut off our food and hit me. That was when Nick got angry. I told him not to... I can take it ... but he kept biting until ... until he grabbed his neck and twisted it broken. ... Nick can't defend himself ... he provoked that man to get himself killed ..." Michael gasped for air.

"He had no right to hit you. For that he would go to jail. But you can't say you'd kill him because of what he did to Nick. I understand you're upset and Nick is your friend ..."

"Is this because Nick is a dog?"

He simply didn't know how to respond without digging deeper into the wound.

"I promised Nick I'm going to get him out of here. I couldn't keep my promise. Without Nick, I can't pick any pockets. Then he beat me more... and more ... just now ... I told him I'm going to kill him. He got angry. He's going to do what he did to Nick. He's going to break my neck tonight. But I'm ready for it... I want to see my mom ..."

Michael swayed, on the verge of passing out. He pulled at the kid and wrapped his arms around him. "When was the last time you ate something?"

"Can't remember ..."

He took off his thick coat and wrapped it around Michael. The coat was too big for the boy to walk in so he carried him in his arms. Michael's head lulled against the crook of his neck and stayed there for a short moment.

He walked along the tunnel to the main road. When he nearly got to the road, Michael stirred and straightened his head. "Where are we going?"

"Hospital. I need to put some food into you, but we have blood all over us. If we go to a food stall, they'll call the cops. So, the hospital seems to be appropriate. I want the doctor to check you out, too."

"No, go to the cops. The police station is just around the corner. We have a dead body in the tunnel and he ain't a dog."

"I can take care of that after I take you to the hospital. I'll call for a car now."

"You mean a cab?"

"No, my company car," he responded, and then remembered he had left his cell phone in the boardroom after the meeting. He must have caused his assistant a panic attack by now. "Damn it!" he cursed.

Michael laughed out loud.

"What's funny?"

"You talk pretty, so I didn't think you'd swear."

"You mean my British accent."

"No. That makes you sound funny. But your words are pretty. I like them. Mom has pretty words, too. She'd been to school for many, many years. She said she wanted me to go to school, too. She never got around to do it. We moved around a lot. Then she ran into him..."

"Did he get violent with your mother?"

Michael said nothing and leaned into the crook of his neck again. "Okay. I won't ask. Now, I don't have my phone with me, so I have to walk to the main road to hail a taxi ..."

"Police station, just around the corner," Michael mumbled.

He kept walking.

"Cabs won't go this way. You can only get them at the rank."

"Would you mind telling me where the rank is? Or I'll go to the main road and ask someone."

"They have food at the police station."

He kept walking.

"You're shaking."

"Yes, I'm cold because you're wearing my coat."

"Okay, you'll find cabs on the left, turn there and cross that little street."

He followed Michael's instructions and ended up at the police station. He pushed the door in. A blast of warm air inside greeted them with the bonus of a dozen pairs of eyes staring at the blood on their clothes.

"Put me down, I look like a scarecrow," Michael said. He put Michael down on the floor and the coat pooled on the floor. Michael took the coat off and gave it back to him.

Seeing the blood, the officer at the front counter gave them immediate attention and got them into an interviewing room, separate from the main foyer.

"Officer, we have an incident to report, but the kid hasn't eaten for days. Could you get him something?"

One officer went for the food and another remained in the interviewing room. The first officer soon returned with a sandwich and a bottle of water.

Before he could say anything, and before the officer took a seat with his notepad, Michael said, "I found him like that in the tunnel. Dead. Blood everywhere. He said he'd get some dinner, but I waited for a long time. So I went out and looked for him. I found him in the tunnel." Then Michael pointed at him, "Then Mr. Pretty Talk found me and took me here. I was scared shitless." Michael bit into the sandwich.

He arched an eyebrow and opened his mouth to say something, but Michael cut in again. "I can sort things out with the officer here. So, you can go now."

"I beg your pardon?" he said.

"The kid said he's fine and you can go. I know the guy Michael's talking about. He's a regular here," the officer said.

"Who's the regular? Michael or his stepfather?"

"Both. His stepfather, if he deserves the title, is the worst kind of junkie. Someone is going to do him in one day. Let's hope today is the day." The officer shook his head and made notes on his writing pad.

"But I found them, shouldn't I give a statement?"

"Ciaran LeBlanc, is it? Sorry if I didn't say your name right." Michael put Ciaran's wallet on the table. "Old habits die hard."

Ciaran smiled. "Now that's pretty talk."

"Mom taught me," Michael grinned. "Didn't mean to pick your wallet. I just wanted to know your name."

"You could have asked me."

Michael took another bite of the sandwich and spoke with a mouth full, "Man, if ya told me, I wouldn't get the spelling right."

"It's shouldn't be a problem if you go to school."

Michael arched an eyebrow. "School doesn't feed me."

"You're saying if you didn't have to worry about food, you would go to school?"

Michael contemplated, but said nothing in response.

"Can you promise me if you don't have to worry about food, you will go to school? I know you're a man of his word."

Michael kept chowing down on the sandwich and shook his head. "I can do this myself. Don't need ya no more." Michael gave Ciaran a dismissive shrug.

Ciaran nodded. "All right then."

He stood up and signaled the officer to take him out. When Ciaran was at the door of the interviewing room, Michael said, "I want more."

Ciaran turned around and arched an eyebrow. "And what else would you like?"

The officer chuckled.

"I go to school, I'll need pocket money. I need to buy clothes, books and all sort of ..."

"All right, you will have an allowance. What else?"

Michael stood up and approached Ciaran. "I will give you your money back and I want it on paper. I want a man to write it down on paper."

Ciaran frowned. "You want me to give you an allowance and have my lawyer put it in writing?"

The officer's jaw dropped and he glared at Michael.

"No. I want your lawyer to write down that I owe you the money and I will pay you back when I grow up. I want to have that paper."

Ciaran nodded. "I'll send my lawyer tomorrow to draw up the paperwork." He glanced at the door of the police station and saw his company car had arrived. Ciaran nodded toward the officer at the counter, thanking him for making the arrangement. Then he turned back to Michael. "I have to go now."

Michael nodded.

"If you want to keep in touch, all you have to do is to ask me. You don't have to hang onto a piece of paper."

"Are you going home now?"

Ciaran nodded. "Yes. I am flying to London tonight."

"When will you be back here?"

"I am not sure. I'll have to check my schedule."

Michael smiled. "See! I need that paper."

Ciaran laughed. "You're a very smart boy. You'll do well at school. Learn everything you can, make a lot of money and pay me back your loan."

"I promise." Michael said solemnly, his eyes gleamed with tears. Ciaran opened his arms. Michael dove in and hugged him.

Ciaran left for the car. Before Ciaran got in, he heard Michael call out. He turned and saw Michael standing at the door of the police station with his palm open, revealing a pocket watch. Michael approached. Ciaran crouched to avoid having his six foot three height towering over Michael.

"I'm sorry. I just wanted a souvenir. Couldn't take this one. It's your father's watch." He gave it back to Ciaran.

Ciaran took the watch, rubbing his thumb on the engraved text, "The love of my life - Conan LeBlanc." He smiled. "I actually stole this from my father."

Michael eyes widened. "You steal?"

Ciaran nodded and winked at Michael.

"Did your father find out?"

Ciaran shook his head.

"You're so cool!"

Ciaran laughed.

"Will you visit me when you come back to New York?"

"Of course, I promise. You can keep this watch if you like, as proof I will be coming back for it."

Michael shook his head. "I have your word and the paper. That's enough. You need that watch more than me."

"What do you mean?"

"In the tunnel, when I said I was ready for him to break my neck, I meant it. Nick was the only thing I had left from my mom and he took Nick from me. When you walked into the tunnel, I saw the light. Mom always said the light would come for me one day, and everything would get better. You brought me the light. I haven't said thank you for that."

"You're welcome." Ciaran smiled and slid the watch back into his pocket.

"Don't let anyone take the watch from you."

"I won't, I promise. Now get back inside, you're shivering."

Michael rushed in and hugged Ciaran tightly one last time, turned on his heel, and then scurried inside the building.

Ciaran stepped into the world of his familiars; inside his long black limousine. As the car left the police station behind, Ciaran saw Michael peeking from inside the door of the police station.

He rubbed his thumb on his pocket watch. His mother had given the watch to his father when they were dating.

If he hadn't stolen the pocket watch off his father, he wouldn't have any personal item from him. The business empire and legacy his father left behind wasn't for him, but for the family. Everything his father had done was to make him a better man and to make the most out of his potential.

But he occasionally wanted to be just a kid, though he knew he was raised for an important cause, whatever it was. He would deal with it when it came his way.

But for now, he was glad Michael had returned the watch. He'd stolen it from his father, and he was still proud of it. He was glad he walked into the tunnel tonight.

He saved the life of a child and, at the same time, had saved a part of his soul.

For all of that, he's grateful.

The End >> Ciaran is the main character in A Shade of Mind and Mindscape series. Information is on the next page.

D.N. LEO 'S NOVELS
SERIES READING ORDER
http://narrativeland.com/dnleonovels/

A SHADE OF MIND
(narrativeland.com/shade)
The Journey from Earth to Eudaiz
Main Characters: Ciaran, Madeline, Tadgh, and Jo
(Recommended reading in order)
1-4 Random Psychic
2-4 Forever Mortal
3-4 Elusive Beings
4-4 Imperfect Divine

—

MINDSCAPE
(narrativeland.com/mind)
Main characters:
Ciaran, Madeline, Tadgh, Jo, Kyle, Hoyt, Ayana, Pete, Sizx, Lorcan, Orla

1-6 Queen's Gambit
2-6 Knight & Pawn
3-6 Lone Castle
4-6 Doubled Bishops
5-6 Dead Squares
6-6 King's Endgame

—

SPECTRUM OF LIES
(narrativeland.com/spectrum)
Main characters: Lorcan, Orla, Roy and Mori
(Recommended reading in order)
1-4 Negotiate Death - White Curse
2-4 Befriend a Rogue - Blue Fox
3-4 Cheat a Sorcerer - Indigo Stone
4-4 Break a Curse - Red Moon

—

SILVER BLOOD
Main characters:
(narrativeland.com/silver)
Ciaran, Madeline, Tadgh, Jo, Caedmon, Sedna,
Roy, Mori, Zach, Mya, Lorcan and Orla

Virgo
Libra
Scorpio
Taurus
Pisces
Gemini

THE GOOD DEITY
Main characters:
(narrativeland.com/deity)
Zach, Mya, Leon, and Kirra
This series can be read in ANY in related to other
series.

Almost Countable
Almost Sure
Almost Everywhere

Thank you for reading.

If you enjoyed reading **The Good Deity 1 - Almost Countable**, I would appreciate it if you would help others enjoy this book, too.

Recommend it. Please help other readers find this book by recommending it to friends, readers' groups and discussion boards.

Review it. Please tell other readers why you liked this book by reviewing it wherever you purchase it. A few sentences will make a significant difference to me. If you do write a review, please send me an email at info@dnleo.com so I can thank you with a personal email.

Connect with me online:
Web: narrativeland.com; Twitter: @dnleostory

Join my mailing list here
http://narrativeland.com/thrills

Facebook page of the Outlanders of the Multiverse series
https://www.facebook.com/Outlandersofthemultiverse

COPYRIGHT

ALMOST COUNTABLE
The Good Deity - Book 1

By D.N. Leo